PRESTO CHANGE-O!

A voice rapped out in metallic tones: "Activate the extruder!"

Though well hidden, I could see by squinting through a crack in the door. Lord Sheba set a small metal tube down on the floor, and slid a translucent ring of some material down over the cylinder. Immediately it began to pulse softly, and then from the open top, what looked like rainbow-colored mud began to flow out on to the floor. There was far more of the stuff than the tube could possibly have contained, and a good-sized blob of it had appeared in a few seconds. Then, just as suddenly, the flow stopped and the tube fell silent.

Abruptly the blob extended itself upward, and then it wasn't a blob any longer.

It was me . . .

THE
PROBABILITY
PAD

THE GREENWICH VILLAGE TRILOGY
BOOK THREE

T. A. WATERS

With a Foreword by
Barbara Hambly

DOVER PUBLICATIONS, INC.
MINEOLA, NEW YORK

Bibliographical Note

This Dover edition, first published in 2019, is an unabridged republication of the work originally printed by Pyramid Books, New York, in 1970.

International Standard Book Number

ISBN-13: 978-0-486-83812-0
ISBN-10: 0-486-83812-9

Manufactured in the United States by LSC Communications
83812901
www.doverpublications.com
2 4 6 8 10 9 7 5 3 1
2019

*This book is for Chester Anderson and Michael Kurland—
and any others whose resemblance to real persons
living or dead is purely coincidental.*

Foreword

I t was Michael Kurland who introduced me to Tom Waters. Twice.

The first time was years before I actually met Michael. It was a central premise of *The Butterfly Kid, The Unicorn Girl,* and *The Probability Pad* that, unlike most stories told from a first person POV, the name of the hero was the same as the name of the author: Hey, this is a book by Chester Anderson and, by gosh, when he talks about "I" he means himself, Chester Anderson, coffeehouse poet and science fiction writer, saving the world from alien invasion. When Michael Kurland narrates his adventures of going on a quest (with his good pal Chester Anderson) with a fair damsel to find her lost unicorn (and ends up saving the multiverse from destruction by intelligent green dinosaurs), he means him, Michael Kurland, retired spy and science fiction author.

And when he speaks of ". . . a tall, thin man in the robes of a mystic, with the erratically trimmed ends of thinning blond hair, sticking out from under his turban . . . ," he means his good friend, magician and mentalist and author T. A. Waters (who in this case had been inexplicably transported to what appeared to be Ogallala, Nebraska, in 1926). Tom later wrote about how he, with the help of his good pals Chester and Michael, also saved the universe. . . .

Even at first reading, I remember being pretty entertained by their descriptions of one another. While Michael is generally described as an ex-spy and self-proclaimed expert on many things, while Tom is always a stage magician and Chester is never without his recorder/hash pipe and his *I Ching*, Chester's description of Michael is rather different than Michael's description of himself.

Both are different from Tom's description of Michael, while Michael sees Tom not quite as Tom sees Tom.

I never did meet Chester Anderson, who passed away shortly before I met Michael Kurland in real life. When the actual Michael Kurland—by that time a friend, living, like me, in Los Angeles—introduced me to the real-life T. A. Waters, Tom looked pretty much exactly like his description. He was at that time the librarian at the Magic Castle, a wonderful restaurant and prestidigitorium on a hill above LA—and also a well-known magician and the author of numerous books on mentalism and stage magic. At this distance, I have little recollection of our conversation, but I do know that I liked him. I subsequently met Tom at several science fiction conventions, and I always enjoyed his company. He was someone I would have liked to know better, and I was saddened to hear of his early death.

But even had I never met any of the intrepid heroes of what later came to be called "the Greenwich Village Trilogy," those three books would still hold a special place in my heart. They were first handed to me in the early 1970s by one of my dojo buddies, and I had never encountered anything like them. But as much as the zany fantasies themselves, it was the world in which they took place that drew me and draws me still. The world of the 1960s. The world I knew.

I suspect it's why *The Probability Pad* is my favorite of the three. It's the shortest and has the simplest plot ("Aliens are attempting to take over the world yet again, how are we going to stop them?"). But while I thoroughly enjoy the others, *The Probability Pad* is the book I've reread the most often. To me, it strongly captures that place, that time.

Yes, all three of the stories take place in some never-quite-defined near-future, wherein it's perfectly okay to smoke pot and become, as Chester says at one point, psychopharmacologically enchanted on a regular and recreational basis. (And to purchase the wherewithal to do so at any drugstore.) Our heroes take it for granted that they have to do occasional reality checks, particularly when the Evil Aliens get stoned and mentally transfer the effects into the brains of our unsuspecting narrators.

I don't think any reader was ever fooled, nor were they intended to be. They take place in the late sixties, and that's the world I remember—the way of looking at the world that I had and my friends had at that weird time when all of us were young. One can almost smell the friendly green whiff of—well, friendly green—mingled with incense, car exhaust, and the moldy scents of cheap New York City lodgings. (That's back when there WERE cheap New York City lodgings.) It's an attitude and a way of looking at the world that went far beyond recreational substances, though they certainly contributed to the ambiance. Well, do I remember having conversations "so vague we couldn't even remember what it was about *during* it. . . ." When at one point Tom describes himself as wearing a neon paisley shirt and op-art jeans, I know that sort of outfit because I saw it on several of my friends. It was a time—and a world—where anything seemed possible and much weirdness was accepted and tolerated.

God knows, I knew enough people who would greet the appearance of a tentacle Chthulhu-like monster with hysterical laughter.

The Probability Pad itself, by the way, is either Michael's Greenwich Village apartment or that of the evil quisling who is selling Earth out to the aliens, Jake Sheba. In either case, the place is familiar: mattresses scattered on the floor of the front room like lily pads (a room looking vainly for an orgy) and assorted six-legged wildlife in the corners. Like the Dude in *The Big Lebowski*, our three heroes give the impression of characters from one type of story who've been dropped into another genre entirely (which also happens several times in the course of the book). Chester, Michael, and Tom slouch amiably through a tale of dark doings, wandering off into conversations with lamps, TV sets, normie tourists from above 14th Street and giant teddy bears (not to speak of guest appearances by Sherlock Holmes, Dracula, and squads of Tiger tanks). Though they're aware that the situation *is* serious (you can't really let Evil Aliens take over the planet), they're not taking any of it particularly seriously.

After all, they've saved the world in the two previous books and are, in fact, getting a little tired of doing so.

As Tom remarks at one point, on the subject of alien invasions of Greenwich Village, "Around here, who would notice?"

To which Chester replies, "Who around here would *care*?"

That, as it turns out, seems to be very much the point, if the book can be said to have one. The baddies are defeated not in battle, but by the fact that nobody takes their invasion seriously. The overly regimented, authoritarian Triskans depend upon disorienting their victims, whom they expect to be exactly like themselves. Confronted by the Village humans' free-form attitude about reality, they are stymied. In a way, it is the human imagination that defeats them—in one of the gentlest climactic battles, perhaps, in all of science fiction.

Like a lot of people, the Triskans just couldn't cope with Flower Power. The sixties leaves them baffled. When anything is possible, nobody is thrown into panic and hysteria at the prospect of the impossible.

In its way, the definition of that place and that time.

That flowers-in-your-hair world couldn't last—if it ever really existed at all—and it was all but gone by the time I first read the books in the much grimmer seventies. But it's good to remember what it was like.

Thank you, Tom, for reaching in and plucking that world out of the time-stream so that we can go back to it for a little while now and then.

—Barbara Hambly
Los Angeles, California
October 2019

FOREWARNED

There is a popular axiom, among those who suffer from an abnormal fear of defining their terms, that anything that is said three times is true.

By anyone, if they lean toward authority figures.

Few people have ever considered me an authority figure—except for my pet cockroaches and erstwhile graduates of Bard College. Nevertheless, and contrariwise, the following Epistle to the Catatonians is sired by *The Butterfly Kid* out of *The Unicorn Girl*, not quite as mixed a marriage as that might sound.

In *The Butterfly Kid*, Chester Anderson told you that none of us were real, and Michael Kurland affirmed our nonexistence in *The Unicorn Girl*.

Ergo, this will be the third time.

Now will you believe it?

1

Time was, as people used to say, and so was reality; things had got back to normal in the Village.

This, the astute reader will realize, is a highly relativistic statement. Both time and reality have always been regarded suspiciously in the Village, and various pharmaceutical concoctions are purveyed to those who wish to circumvent them. Such natural leanings sometimes complicate things, such as the Reality Pills and the Time Bubble bath.

There are situations, however, when this perversity of Village/hippie/mod/beat/uncertain types can be their saving grace. The saving of all of us, I learned, and this was the way of it . . .

It was the spring after the Time Bubble. Having saved humanity for the second time, Chester and Michael were in a state of Extreme Smug. I could've copped a little Smug myself, having had a hand in the second of these adventures, but there had been so many side issues of varying morality that I had opted to abstain completely.

A guilty bystander, as it were.

Michael sauntered into the Pentalpha, our replacement hangout after the Garden of Eden had been crated up and sent to Marrakech, along with its manager. He squinted through the emptiness toward the stage where I was sitting.

"Look!" he cried to the lack of audience. "Waters is holding his ball!"

"That's the thirty-seventh time, Michael," I reminded him gently, and hefted the prop crystal experimentally.

Hmm?

No, I decided regretfully. I had to have the crystal for my mindreading act. I presented—exhibited would be a better word—a combination of blab and chicanery every night at the Pentalpha. It was my then successful method of avoiding work, and gave me a curious reputation quite superior to some of my prior curious reputations.

Michael Kurland, former spy, raconteur, bookie, editor, NBC vassal—Michael, currently *very* freelance writer—Michael the Theodore Bear/M.T. Bear, the Empty Bear—Michael sat down.

"Hot," he pronounced.

"Very hot," he expanded, quite understandable to those with a scientific turn of mind.

"Don't," he contracted when I brandished a diet tamarindo ice at him. "I'm giving up everything I can't stand for Lent."

I drank it myself, as penance for having failed to foist it off on Michael. It wasn't nearly as bad as I had intended it to be; I felt doubly cheated.

"Chester," said Michael, eyeing the glare of spring sunlight beyond the windows as though it were part of a plot against him, "has disappeared."

"He might have gone above Fourteenth Street," I suggested as an alternative. Village types are very provincial.

Michael shook his eyes, apparently because shaking his head was beyond him at the moment. "You don't understand," he said, "I mean *disappeared* disappeared."

"You mean poof like that disappeared?"

Michael's eyes nodded.

"Into thin air? Optical wipe? Blip?"

The eyes confirmed this.

"Michael, what're you on?"

The eyes faced each other for a moment to make some sort of agreement, and then reset to triangulate on me. "You know me better than that; I never have anything stronger than Chemex with Jello. Why not ask Chester what *he's* on? He's the one that disappeared."

I could see that Michael was a bit shook, since logic was usually his strong suit.

"Where did this special effect take place?" Urgh! The tamarindo was beginning to turn on me.

"Down at the loft on Broome Street." Michael seemed to come out of the slight trance, and went into his Occurrences, Unusual, Reporting Of voice. "I woke him up about an hour ago, since I know how to get around his Vidiphone null circuit, and went over to pick him up. After two fugues on the electric harpsichord and a bit of Vivaldi on the recorders I finally got him moving. We were heading down the last flight—the one to the main landing—Chester was in front of me."

"And?" I prodded.

"Blip."

"Blip?"

"Blip. He just wasn't there any more. There was only afternoon where there had been all of Chester."

I tried the unlikely suggestion. "Do you suppose Chester pulled some sort of stunt on you as revenge for bestirring him while the sun was still up?"

"There isn't a gimmick made that could produce that effect, and you, as an *ex-jongleur,* damn well know it," Michael grumped. "Besides"—he made a professorial gesture—"it just isn't Chesterian. Too un-subtle for him, just ceasing to be like that."

"Quit copping from old Saint stories," I said sternly, "and let me go down there and take a look around." It was a bit annoying to think that a neophyte in the field like Chester could pull off so baffling a trick. I was still thinking in these terms and wasn't going to give up so easily.

Michael's watch told him, in a dull monotone, that it had only been twenty minutes since Minus Chester—not much time to move the kind of props you'd need, but there was no sign of wires, mirrors, or laser holograms. It was certainly puzzling. We moped about and shook our heads for some time, and then I finally gave up. If Chester really *had* disappeared, he'd done it in a way that was Unknown To Modern Science.

About fifteen feet later Michael suddenly stopped and put his hands gingerly out from his sides, as though feeling for an antique hula hoop.

"It'll never fly," I offered.

"Quiet." Michael gave me his Force Two glower. "I'm trying to think."

Overcoming the temptations that this straight line presented occupied me for some moments, until, "the bannister."

"What?"

"The bannister," Michael repeated, saying it louder and more truculently so I would understand. "The railing. There was one on the wall side of the stairs as well as the well side."

"So?" Monosyllables were my *forte* that year.

"There was never a railing on the wall side before."

We raced back into the building.

There was no extra railing now, but a serpentine dust trail wound down to the landing from the wall at the upper end. We gazed at this for some time in silence.

"Disappearing Chester," I moped.

"Appearing and disappearing railings," Michael fretted.

"What," we chorused at each other in unison, "does it all *mean?*"

We were so irrationally pleased with the dramatic effect of this that we started to do a shuffle-off-to-Buffalo back out on to Broome Street. At this point, during our momentary silence, The Sound came from above.

As sounds go, it wasn't particularly loud; no, its paralytic quality lay in the fact that it was something that neither of us had ever heard before, but which we could quite clearly identify.

Michael looked up at the ceiling, the source of The Sound, and then back at me. "No," he said after what was for us an almost indecent pause. "No, it's your turn—you'll have to say it."

"It sounded," I finally admitted to myself, Michael and the cockroaches, "—it sounded like a stair railing crawling across a floor."

2

We were getting very good at pauses.

This one, while not quite pregnant, had certainly been fooled around with. It was a full ten seconds, with that indescribable skitter-sliding above us, before we broke formation and raced upstairs. I noted abstractedly that I was in the lead. This seemed to happen often in these situations, and I'm still not quite sure whether it was stupidity or ambition.

Just before I reached the second landing a new and much noisier clatter reached our ears, which we were still (spookily) able to interpret as the railing climbing? crawling? hopping? up the next flight of stairs. And me with only a tamarindo . . .

At the fourth floor there was no sound, and no extra railing. It had quite efficiently given us whatever a railing would call the slip.

"Humiliating," said Michael.

"A railing managing to lose two ex-spies of our caliber."

"What will people *say*?"

"Who," I asked, "is going to tell them?"

Michael smiled, for the first time that day. "A touch," he said, "a very distinct touch."

We wended our way back toward the Pentalpha. It was a lengthy wend, for Michael encountered one of his paramours-in-progress on Houston Street. I stood by silently counting gas stations while he went through his catalogue of ploys. He had reached Ploy G, Variant III when I ran out of petroleum outlets, and I tapped him unobtrusively on the shoulder. "What about Chester?"

Michael gnurphed and grumped, but my interjection had broken his dramatic flow, and I knew he wouldn't be up to starting again. Nameless Uptown Girl went through an elaborately mimed goodbye, and disappeared stage left toward Broadway.

"You're interfering with what could've been some very nice sublimating," Michael muttered as we trudged up Sullivan Street.

"The least of our worries." We rounded the corner and headed for the inviting coolness of the Pentalpha. "We spend the morning—the afternoon—chasing railings, and unsuccessfully at that, after your

> dearest
> oldest
> strangest
> most ephemeral
> none of the above
> (check one)
>
> friend

disappears before your very eyes, and all you can think about is the gratification of your base desires."

"It wasn't all that base," Michael explained, "she'd read all my books."

"Oh." This put an entirely different light on the matter.

I now felt properly sad and ashamed about having deprived Michael of an Audience. Audiences for writers, which can consist of as few people as one and usually do, are essential to a leisurely and pleasured way of life. If the writer is without an Audience to marvel at the galaxy of *bon mots* that flow from his lips in endless profusion, there is really little left that he can do except write—actually write—which is rather an extreme solution to the problem.

We two-by-twoed into the Pentalpha and stopped short, a position we were getting used to.

Sitting on the stage, briefcase and notebooks forming a protective wall about him, and playing *The Carman's Whistle* on his battle-scarred alto recorder, was Chester Anderson.

He looked quite as though he hadn't been disappearing much at all, and both Michael and I felt this to be somewhat inconsiderate.

"Ah, Michael, Thomas. I have been awaiting you."

"That isn't all you've been doing," Michael growled.

"True," confirmed Chester. "I have also been (a) doing some *I Ching* correlations, (b) plotting the final volume of our octology, (c) trying to obtain some hashish of at least middling quality—the level has certainly gone down since the stuff became legal, (d) looking for Steve Netley, who's supposed to use some of these arrangements in his barock group, (e) plotting social revolution, and therefore (f) putting *The Carman's Whistle* into march time."

"And disappearing," I appended.

"Ah, hmm?" Chester looked from me to Michael and back, apprehending that something might be a bit amiss. After all, it had been fully thirty seconds since our arrival and we hadn't yet done even one Thirties vaudeville bit.

"Where did you go this morning?" asked Michael in intelligence-officer high style.

"To the Bridgeport monorail station," Chester replied equably. "When I arrived in Manhattan there were a few things I had to do uptown, and then I came down here about—" Chester had a short colloquy with his watch—"about twenty minutes ago. Guilty or Not Guilty?"

"Not Guilty, by reason of uncertainty," I offered, to cover from any available audience the fact that I was as rattled as Mike. These were deep waters, and so was I.

"You mean," Michael said, filling out an old Department of Defense form in his head, "that you haven't been here all day? You weren't at your loft this morning?"

Chester did a Thunder-And-Lightning trill on the recorder, and broke off to give my fellow interrogator a professorial peer. He turned to me. "Is Michael by any chance psychopharmacologically enchanted?"

"Don't ask me. I've been spending the day chasing stair railings."

"Oh."

We gave Chester a rundown on the events of the day in which he hadn't apparently figured, using our best *stichomythia* method of presentation. His eyes swung back and forth as we talked, somewhat like a lethargic tennis spectator.

"Someone's been imitating *me*?" he asked at the conclusion of our Huntley-Brinkley presentation.

"It seems that way," said Michael, "unless you were dreaming that you were in Bridgeport or we were dreaming that we were here."

"But we *are* here," I reminded Michael. It was quite possible that in view of the day's events he had chosen to forget. "Besides, even if Chester was here that still wouldn't explain how he could've not been here when he vanished." I was proud at being able to spot Michael's error of logic.

"How's that again?" Mike wasn't quite ready to concede the point.

"Someone's been *imitating* me," stated Chester, as though for the benefit of a reporter from the *Encyclopedia Britannica*.

People had begun to drift in from the Midway, our code term for the Third Street-MacDougal-Bleecker area, and I ushered a genuinely bewildered Mike and a genuinely genuine Chester into the back room. A single lumipanel lit the room, and for this we were thankful; our manager had the idea that sanitation was a Communist plot.

There were strange electronic twangings beginning to filter in from the front as we sat down to talk; Piltdown and His Primates, our then house barock group, was tuning up. After a particularly tortuous sequence of semi-ascending chords from Piltdown's guitar there was scattered applause from the audience, some of whom were under the impression that he'd just finished an experimental solo.

Michael suddenly jumped up from his seat. A cockroach, poised in the center of the chair, glared up at him and moved its antennae threateningly. Then, possibly thinking of some more devious revenge, it stomped off.

There are people, I understand, who have never lived on the Lower East Side or in the Village, and who therefore are disinclined to believe that a cockroach can stomp. Hard to believe. But I digress . . .

"*Someone's* been imitating me," Chester stated flatly, glancing around in steely paranoia.

There was a pause, while the three of us listened to the leaden footfalls of the departing cockroach. Then Michael took the floor, and he was welcome to it.

"It's a plot." Michael always laid his groundwork carefully. "It's a plot, and it breaks itself down into a number of subdivisions, *i.e.,* (a) who's doing it? (b) why are they doing it to *us?* (c) *cui,* as they yet may be saying in detective stories, *bono?* AND (d) why Chester, of all people?"

"I am not at all sure that either pleasure or annoyance should be my response to your point (d)," said Chester, "and I will therefore let it pass." He was fitting a brass mouthpiece on to one end of the recorder and a little screened bowl on to the other. "That (c) on the other hand is certainly suggestive. I can't imagine anyone we either know or could conceive of going to this much trouble for the sake of a bit of obscurantist humor. We could therefore assume that whatever this whole thing is, it isn't connected with any of us directly, and that the fact that this *ersatz* whatever-it-was happens to be an *ersatz* me is but a result of random selection."

Michael disagreed. "For our mystery people to be able to duplicate so exactly just anybody they happened to encounter would take a hell of a technology, with techniques like nothing on Earth."

"Like nothing on Earth," I echoed, and the two of them turned to stare at me.

"Uh—uh. Nertz. Gnurph," said Michael.

"I refuse," said Chester, "I absolutely refuse."

"Well, it was only a thought," I said. "After all, by this time we could think of it as traditional. And another point; we know it's happened at least once before, and it might have happened more often than that—invasion, that is. I mean, around here, who would notice?"

"Several people might," said Chester, "such as us. The real point is, who around here would *care?*"

Pause number 40-A-3, with us all thinking that one over for a bit. We were interrupted at our devotions by the King of the Gnomes, as we called the manager of the Pentalpha, who came back to tell me that a passel of the faithful had managed to endure a set of Piltdown and his group—or mob—and it was time for me to do the mindreading bit. "Working the ball" was what the manager called it, and my head was so far out in those days that it was some time before I realized he was referring to the crystal. Strange, strange. I dropped the ring-mike over my head and went out onto the stage to survey the somewhat choppy sea of faces.

"Down through the dim corridors of time, man has sought to pierce the veil that hides him from the future. There have been a fortunate few who have looked into the crystal and have *seen*. Is it some property of the crystal globe itself, or does the seer but use it to turn his vision inward? No one knows—but the visions come, the visions come . . ." I said.

"But hold! The shifting shapes begin to clear. An image forms, of a lady mature in years and wisdom, who has recently suffered a grave loss. I receive the initials G.R.L.—is someone with those initials sending me a telepathic message?"

A woman in late middle age with a dead fox around her throat raised her hand unsteadily, and heroically tried to focus on me.

"Don't say a word, Madam, just let me sense your thoughts—ah, yes, the loss we're thinking of was a pet . . . a small dog . . . concentrate . . . yes, it's becoming clearer now . . . you found him strung up to the top of your flagpole on the Fourth of July last, correct? Madam, I know you would wish to find the perpetrator of this foul deed, but I'm not permitted to give any sort of information of the type you seek. However, I can tell you this; it was someone jealous of you, of your suavity, maturity, your personality—and it can certainly be said that this person is not very patriotic."

I went on like this for what seemed like hours but was, Michael and Chester assured me, only twenty minutes. Finally it was over and the three of us scurried out as soon as I had begged off doing the later show. I was suffering from excessive reality poisoning, and only getting back to our little pseudo-Chester problem would do anything to break my funk. We descended into the Cafe Nobody and headed for the back.

As it happened, we didn't have to do any hunting for our little problem; it came to us in the form of Wendy West, sometime folksinger and friend to man, if he was her type. Wendy tromped over to the table and glowered down at us. "You two!" she snarled at me and Michael, "you're really quite something, aren't you?" She turned to Chester. "I don't mean you—but these two . . . !"

Since none of us now had any idea who was being complimented or denigrated, Chester in particular, I lodged a formal protest. "Michael's the cryptographer. Could you tell *me* what all this is in aid of?"

"I just didn't like the way you two ignored me completely this morning on Second Avenue," answered Wendy. "I was with another girl and it was somewhat embarrassing."

Michael knew full well that the table had nothing to do with all this, but he beat on it anyway. "You saw Thomas and me on Second Avenue today? This morning?"

Chester chortled in high glee. "Welcome to the club," he sardonicized, and played a little taradiddle on the recorder; not the easiest thing, since the bowl and pipe mouthpiece were still attached to it.

"You're sure that it was us?" I tried. "Not just people who looked like us from a distance?"

"Positive." Wendy plopped down in my lap and began to nuzzle me, too pleasantly to be called distracting. "And who knows what you look like better than me?" added her tongue from somewhere inside my ear.

"If you two will stop that exhibitionist foreplay for a while," said Chester, "perhaps we can get somewhere with this. It now appears that there are at least three duplicates that we know of, and those only by chance or direct contact. There may be droves of imitation people in the Village for all we know."

"It would hardly be a change from the old days," said Michael.

"Very funny. Let's set a precedent and try to approach this thing logically. You two are supposed to be the ex-spies, so you can do the legwork." The logic of this was lost on us for the moment, but Mike and I said nothing. "I will go at it from the other end, and construct a philosophical system that explains it."

"Right," I affirmed. "And then I'll do the book and Mike the lyrics, and with any luck at all we should have it on Broadway by October."

"Not me," said Michael. "I can't think of a single rhyme, offhand, for transmogrify. Besides, what we need at the moment is a base of operations."

"Your apartment," Chester and I said simultaneously and only a half-tone apart.

Michael thought of objecting but decided against it. For one thing, it meant that Chester and I would have to do most of the walking, getting to Michael's cleverly hidden pad, and that in turn meant that Mike could sleep longer. Sleeping was a periodic hobby of Michael's, and he did it so well that Chester had once threatened* to write a book about it. He got about three chapters in and then dropped the project. "I kept falling asleep," Chester explained.

There was also the inducement that he'd be able to set up a War Room. Michael was quite a student of war, and War Rooms in particular, and he hadn't had one since he'd left the Army because his personal wars were generally over too quickly to make it worthwhile.

Michael announced that he would go home forthwith and set up the Operations Office; he had to go home anyway, because he had a deadline to meet on an adventure novel. (This was true; of course, the deadline was a date two months earlier, but like me, Mike considered deadlines in financial rather than chronological terms.)

Chester had settled down to work on his notebooks; his recorder-*cum*-hashish pipe was now lit, and the smoke came out of all the little holes and produced the effect of a dematerializing harp.

So I extracted Wendy from my ear long enough to get us back to the pad, and things were nice.

After all, Rome wasn't torn down in a day, either.

---

* Chester Anderson, *The Butterfly Kid* (Mineola, New York: Dover Publications, 2019), pp. 88-89.

3

could tell that it was morning; the sky was a dirty yellow instead of a dirty pink.

I rolled over on nothing, and cleverly deduced that Wendy had already split. It was a habit of hers; nights were for people, but days were for her cats and her guitar. An interesting quirk, but I never knocked it, for who among us had such an ordered life?

After taking a cold shower, because that was the only kind of water there was, I got dressed and buzzed Mike.

Blear. "New York Contagious Diseases Hospital, may I help you?"

"Hgh argh thgs whig khnoo hrhss mrgng?"

"Um?"

"I covered my mouth while speaking. How are things with you this morning?"

"Things are interesting." Michael put on his Ominous Revelation voice. "Come on over. I have something to show you."

"What?" I said, knowing that I would find out when I got over there.

"You'll find out when you get over here."

See?

"Um. Do you have anything to eat over there?"

"Everything you could possibly desire—Pepsi and peanut butter."

"Cupcakes?"

"Two out of three," said Michael, "but get over here anyway. Chester's here, and so is the mystery object."

It took longer than I had expected to get over to Michael's, since we were already in the throes of an invasion; people from

Queens and the Bronx, trying to find Greenwich Village while
they were in the middle of it, and then, on discovering it, getting
the look of people at a sideshow who find out that the two-
headed baby is a stuffed one that floats in a jar.

Michael's front-room floor was studded with mattresses, like
lily pads in a pond, a room looking vainly for an orgy. Mike was
pinning a map of the lower East Side to one wall, and Chester
was fiddling with his recorder pipe. "Catch," he said when I
came in, and tossed it in my general direction—not a Chester
gesture.

"So?" I said.

"That's Exhibit A," said Chester. He reached into his briefcase and extracted an exact duplicate of what I was holding.

The two recorders were so alike that their own mother
couldn't have told them apart—a metaphor that was beginning
to assume the proportions of reality. Whatever this thing from
Outer Wherever was, it apparently had the ability to become the
Mother Of Us All—or at least the mother of our identical twins.

What, as Michael and I had remarked not too long before, did
it all mean?

I looked at them until the novelty wore off, and then turned to
Chester. "Which one is which?"

He was making marks on Michael's wall map. Anyone else
would've used x's or check marks, but Chester was drawing in
little Maltese crosses in green ink. Glancing up, he said "the one
in your—uh—"

There was a curious special effect at this point, which can only
be described if you imagine Chester to be made of plaster of
Paris; it seemed, to the detached observer (me), that he seemed to
bubble slightly and harden.

"Thomas," he said, illuminating his words with a jeweled
intensity, "I have had that recorder pipe for a *terribly* long time.
Since before I could use it in public without getting busted, as
a matter of fact. As season gave way to season through many
years it comforted me in its sundry ways. You are now, really and
seriously, telling me that you couldn't keep track of it for thirty
seconds?"

It was my finest hour. "Ah—er—uh—mmm . . ."

"Hold it," said Mike, and not a moment too soon, because I was running out of noncommittal grunts. "Don't get excited, Chester. This may turn out to be a good thing; after all, there have to be *some* points of difference between the real one and the fake, don't there?"

Chester didn't say a word and I said the same thing.

"Right," said Michael, cheered by our support. "So when we figure out just what it is that makes one of the duplicates different, then we'll have a test that we can apply to all of them."

This sounded logical, which in itself should have warned us, but we agreed anyway.

"Right," Michael repeated. "Let's get to work."

THE CURTAIN IS LOWERED FOR SIX HOURS TO DENOTE THE PASSAGE OF ONE-FOURTH OF A DAY.

"Any other ideas?" I inquired.

Michael glared at the two recorders as though they were committing something out of the *Ananga Ranga,* "There's got to be *some* point of difference," he insisted, getting up and rubbing his eyes.

Chester looked up from the notebook he had been filling all afternoon.

"Why?" he asked.

Since the mix-up had been my fault, I decided to take an ethical stand. "Yeah, Mike, why?"

"Well . . . for it to be an exact duplication, it would have to be done atom by atom."

"So?" I countered. "You said yesterday that it would take a technology like nothing on Earth, and what the hell do we know about extraterrestrial technology?"

Michael shook his head. "I'm not going to get into that thing again. Maybe last year invasions from outer space were in vogue, but I've had it with 'em. Let the Aliens pick on somebody else for a change. I, for one, absolutely refuse."

"*I* refuse," echoed Chester.

"Same here," said Chester. Michael and I spun around and goggled.

It was comforting to realize that the whole thing hadn't been a weird joke, and that we were somewhat in touch with reality; but this occurred to us only in retrospect. For the moment we were a somewhat paralyzed quartet; me, Mike, Chester, and Chester.

The tableau held for about ten seconds; then one of the Chesters walked over to the desk and picked up a recorder. "I believe this is mine," he said, and walked out.

It was a few seconds before either Mike or I could recover. We raced out into the hall but it was, to nobody's surprise, empty of anything except a smell of decayed urine. This particular odor is peculiar to the buildings of certain areas of Manhattan, along with subscents of old newspaper, boiled cabbage, socks, and cheap laundries.

We went back into the pad to face Chester, who was now holding the other recorder. "I suppose," he said, looking up, "that this must be the original."

"Yes—" I said, and stopped. Mike and I looked at Chester for some time before he realized what was going through our heads.

"Gentlemen, please," he protested, "if *I* were the fake then why would I leave?" He stopped for a moment. "I mean, if the *me* that you see were a fake, why would the *real* me have left for no reason? Let's not make things any more complicated than they are." I looked at Michael. "He has a point." "Gnurph. We'll have to accept him on trust, for now anyway."

The vidiphone buzzed, and while Chester continued his now needless protestations I went into the other room to answer it. An illegal interconnecting cord ran from its socket to, predictably, a table by the bed. Mike could answer it without having to actually be awake, and this began to explain some of the strange phone conversations I'd been having with him lately.

It was the manager of the Pentalpha. "I thought I'd find ya here, ya bum. You forgot you still working for me?"

I prodded my watch and it petulantly informed me that it was past eight in the evening. The windows had been dark for some time, but I had subconsciously taken this to be the New York air descending on them. "Sorry. I'll be over in a few minutes. I didn't know what the time was."

"Hah! Some mindreader!" The screen went dark.

I went back into the other room. "The plot against the world in general and us in particular is going to have to wait for a liddy bit. I have to go do my thing."

"I thought you'd *done* your thing," said Chester.

"I did, but the operation didn't take. Anyway, I'll see you both in the Nobody after I'm finished."

"Groovy."

"Groovy?"

"I read it somewhere," said Mike shamefacedly.

Walking across town from the Lower East Side to the Village was still something of an adventure on temperate evenings. There were the inevitable teenagers playing incomprehensible stickball games on the street, and a number of these games seemed to involve the statutory rape of a ten or eleven-year-old girl, as part of the proceedings, but whether this was supposed to be a bonus or a handicap I had never been able to figure out. Whole families had surrendered their apartments to the roaches for the evening and descended *en masse* to the front stoop for riotous conclave, beer drinking, plotting against whatever minority group they didn't belong to, and other amusements. Civic Theater-in-the-Streets rarely got down to this neck of the woods, but we weren't without entertainment; there were at least three bums and two psychos per block, and they made a point of performing for any available audience. One of the lines that year was "Pardon me, Sir, but I just murdered my mother and I need a cup of coffee to steady myself," and there were other variants fully as hilarious. It amused some people—the sort of people who would have described the area as quaint and picturesque—but it only made me nervous.

Everybody seemed to be in show business; what the hell had happened to the audience?

One of the show-biz bums accosted me; I said, "Tanarg frag sajili helepas" to him and he veered away. Bums are above all else pragmatists and it was evident I was a bad bet to begin with. I hardly noticed it anyway, because I was stewing.

There was something wrong here; not odd, because to say something was odd in our enchanted kingdom was not exactly a descriptive term. No, this was *wrong,* because I had the uncanny feeling that there were a lot of things happening that I wasn't aware of; some sort of gigantic plot that everybody was in on but me. It just didn't seem that enough was happening.

Fat chance.

I stopped at the Jewel Bar, a soda fountain on Second Avenue near St. Marks Place that was notable for its milkshakes and its use as a mail room for the Syndicate. Elbowing through the forest of black shirts and white silk ties, I finally got to the counter and ordered an egg cream.* It didn't do my stomach any good, something it had in common with my prospects for the evening.

Then, as luck would have it (an interesting phrase: one is immediately tempted to ask, when that particular set of words is used, Whose Luck?), I ran into Amy Muscar.

Amanda Muscar, and she insisted that was her name in spite of the botanists among us, was something of a fixture around the Village. She had been a friend of Doc Dee, the charismatic drug guru, back in the days before hallucinogens became legal and thus lost, for a great segment of the Village population, their chiefest charm. The Doc had disappeared, and for a while Amy had enjoyed the mystique of being one of his grieving mistresses, in spite of the fact that this was not exactly a distinction held by a few.

The novelty had finally worn off, and Amy had taken to collecting and cataloging whatever young male flesh came (you should pardon the expression) into range. Catalogue was the word, too; her little card file, arranged alphabetically by age, machinery size and favored technique, was something of a legend in the village, though only a few people had seen it. One was an acquaintance of mine who, after reading her critique of him, suffered quite a deflation of ego—among other things.

I wasn't on the card file as of this moment, due more to circumstance than anything else. Amy was nearly thirty, but the hip-huggers and see-through blouse she wore made her abundant charms abundantly evident. I decided to be scintillating.

"And how are you today?" Scintillating.

---

* egg cream—a vile concoction that has neither egg nor cream.

Amy looked at me with a broad's smile. "Who should know better than you, after last night?"

"AARGH!" I bought a copy of the *News,* leafed through it, and ate it.

"What's the matter with you?" cried Amy as I stuffed the last of the Sports section into my mouth. I'd finished it all but the editorial page, which I never had been able to stomach.

"How was I?" It seemed a fair question.

Amy moved back a step. "Uh—you were fine, just fine." I growled and snorted. "Why? Is anything the matter?"

"If you should run into Wendy," I said, "I suggest you ask her that question. You may discover I have talents not even you have suspected." I tromped away, leaving Amy standing there in a puzzled stance. On her it looked good, but I was in no mood to appreciate it.

MacDougal Street, though neither round, firm, nor free and easy on the draw, was fully packed, and it took a bit of wending before I was finally able to dodge into the Pentalpha. Piltdown and the Primates were on, which meant I'd missed my first set, and I didn't particularly relish facing the manager, but Greed Conquers All. He was in his packrat nest behind the cash register, and as I approached he looked up warily, probably suspecting that I was going to steal one of his shiny objects.

"Sorry about what happened," I tried, "but—"

"Sorry? Why sorry? Didn't you like the way the first set went?"

And to think I'd been feeling sorry for Chester. Dreamily I asked my fair question.

"You were fine, I thought," responded Weinie, and the lovely *deja vu* was really beginning to whack me out

"Riiiiiiiiiiight! See you later." Perhaps Michael and Chester would be in the Nobody, though it was still early. If they weren't, I would just stay there and wait for them, I would . . .

Things *were* getting strange.

I stopped at the corner to wait for the light. I waited for it a long time but it never showed up, so I decided to go in without it. Silly light, standing me up. I'd show it.

I hadn't been this high in years, and I was surprised at how pleasant it seemed. Of course, somewhere inside my head there was this idiot named Waters trying to tell me that something was wrong, that I shouldn't be feeling this good, but he was just a dumb old spoilsport and what did he know, anyway?

Now *there* was a good question. I examined it in all its aspects and ramifications for about three hundred years, during which time the doorway of the Nobody slid along the wall to my left. Finally it jumped in front of me and swallowed me, and I stopped in its trachea to see if Michael and Chester were in its stomach.

It didn't take my eyes long to get accustomed to the murkiness; they were already so dilated, I noted in the mirror behind the bar, that I could have done a creditable imitation of a tarsier.

Ah, yes, there they were, down at the entrance to the large intestine. It was a good thing that they hadn't been digested; I congratulated myself on my remarkable good luck.

I settled down at the wooden table and greeted them pleasantly. "I'm glad to see that you two haven't been dissolved by all these stomach acids," I said, It seemed the polite thing to say but for some reason Michael and Chester both were apparently bothered by it.

They held a mute colloquy of shrugs, eye-rollings, headnodding and shaking, and whistles, amidst a general air of disapprobation.

After a while of this Chester turned to me. "It appears, Thomas, that you have got yourself chemically entranced. In view of the situation, may Michael and I ask why?"

It was an awfully long question, but I should try to answer it, I felt; somebody in me was insisting that it was important that I make some sort of stab at communication.

"That's what's so interesting," I said over what seemed to be a period of several hours. "You see, I haven't taken anything. I was over at the Pentalpha and found out that I'd already done my set—the other me had done it, that is—and I was perfectly fine then. Everyone kept saying that, that I was perfectly fine, and it wasn't even me. But I me me was fine too, until I started coming over here, and then things started acting very peculiar."

"You didn't eat or drink anything?" Michael asked.

It didn't take quite as long to answer that one; I was already beginning to come down. "Just an egg cream at the Jewel and a copy of the *Daily News*."

The answer seemed to satisfy them, and there was silence for a few seconds. Then Mike stood up abruptly, wearing his Superspy-strikes-again look. "I have an idea," he said. "Keep an eye on Tom while I check around a few places I know. I'll be back in less than an hour."

Three hours later, on the dot, Michael reappeared. His arrival reminded me that I hadn't gone back to the Pentalpha to do my second set, and I wondered whether my accommodating twin had filled in for me. At this point my lucubrations were thrown off track by a blonde in a fishnet dress swiveling by, and it occurred to me that duplicate Thomas might be following more rewarding courses.

Michael looked very pleased. "I was right," he crowed. "You bought a capsule of Ambrosine at Washington Drugs earlier this evening."

"Categorically no."

"There's only one category," Michael charitably pointed out. "I don't mean you, anyway, I mean the fake you."

"Then why did *I* get whacked out?"

"That was my theory." Michael was back in smug again for the first time since yesterday morning. "Now we've decided," he continued, "that whatever this is, it can produce exact duplications, atom for atom, down to the brain cells, which is why they seem to know everything about us that we do, right? And they must be able to exert some sort of mind-over-matter control to be able to change shapes. So here's this exact duplicate of you, which, in checking through your habits, tries something that you've used on occasion, Ambrosine, and for some reason he can't take it—or it can't, or whatever. So it transfers the stuff to the only other structure that can hold it in whatever configuration the fake body has shaped it, which is to say, *you*. Presto, you're high."

It was insane and utterly preposterous, and there were other points in its favor as well. The theory fit all the facts, and it at least gave us a base to start working from—better than anything we had up to now. Chester and I agreed to accept it provisionally, the provision simply being that neither of us were going to accept any responsibility for what happened if we found a way to act on it.

Things began to get interesting and the evening, which hadn't promised much, was delivering. Apparently word had got round about what was happening, and people started dropping by our table to add little bits and pieces to what we had.

We weren't the only people that were being duplicated; a whole section of the Village and the Lower East Side had been the focus for bogus bohemians. It was quite evident that most of the people who talked to us were pretty relieved at finding out they hadn't freaked-out completely, and we got a great mass of information as the hours passed.

It was interesting, but it didn't help us much.

Michael and Chester took copious notes while all this was going on; listening was hard enough work for me. Not only people, but objects had been duplicated; Chester's pipe recorder had not been a fluke. Bottles, flowers, puppies, bookcases, vibrators—about anything you could think of had been copied at least once. There was a new aspect to the operations of the Aliens (we'd given up and decided to use that as a label) that we discovered as the reports progressed. They weren't limited to duplicating. Some people reported the appearance of more or less common objects—rugs, doors, etc.—that weren't like anything they owned. If they noticed it, the object vanished as soon as they took their eyes off it.

One of the last people to come waltzing up to our High Court table was Mystic Jake; it was at this point, exactly, that we had decided to use the term *Alien*—anything that could or would duplicate Mystic Jake would *have* to be Alien.

Mystic Jake Sheba was one of those people of whom it may truly be said that if he hadn't existed someone would have had to invent him. The reason was that he filled a need, though any society that needed him was already in trouble.

Mystic Jake was a promoter, a wheeler-dealer, an arranger of things. He was the power behind some of the big names in barock music. He was on speaking terms with the media bigwigs, first-name basis of course, and could predict the course of pop music for years to come.

So he said.

Mystic Jake was, first of all, neither Mystic nor Jake; it was common knowledge that he had adopted the name Jake Sheba to avoid certain bothersome legal proceedings, and the Mystic part had been contributed by Chester some years before and referred to function rather than form—most of Mystic Jake's world was in his head, as harrowing a place as you could wish for.

In form Jake was a Persian cat turned used-car dealer; there was a puffy sleekness about him that put all but the most ingenuous on guard; unfortunately the Village had always had a healthy supply of youthful ingenuousness, and Jake's ability to locate it was that of a homing vampire.

He took pride in his appearance, which was a good index of his aesthetic abilities. For as long as anyone could remember Jake had worn Italian silk suits—two of them—and pointed shoes. The result was that a few young musicians with more talent than brains had figured that his rather bizarre appearance, by Village standards, meant that he was successful; the uptown bookers and moguls figured him for a loser and no longer even bothered to answer his calls; and Mystic Jake collected his twenty-five percent of their coffeehouse and club earnings and told them to keep preparing for the big break.

Through no fault of Jake's this wasn't entirely false; his clients did get a break of sorts, whenever they wised up and quit him for another agent—any other agent.

It was just one of those things—as the song goes—Mystic Jake had become a fixture around the Village, and the situation was sort of like a lovely camping ground with a quicksand bed; you enjoyed the view and the advantages, and when you could you tried to keep others from stepping into the mud and sinking out of sight. It had been the same with Laszlo Scott until the Bard of MacDougal Street was borne away amidst a clack of blue crustaceans, and it would probably be the same if ever Jake disappeared. Every silver lining, as the other song goes, has a cloud.

And now Jake was telling us, in story and what might theoretically be song, about his encounter with said Alien. He had, he told us, been on his way up to General Morris Agency to sign the final contracts for his hot new group, when he saw his double walking along Second Avenue. Jake ran after it, but it spotted him and lost him after a heroic four-block run.

Normally our limit with Mystic Jake would have been three words—one each for Chester, Mike, and me—but one could never tell what might be important so we let him go through it. Luckily he had an important deal pending (at four in the morning?) so we didn't have to go through one of our standard routines designed to get rid of him.

Finally we were alone except for the bartender and Annie, one of Nobody's owners. She served us tasty sustenance, avoiding trial gropes with the skill of a *torero*, and then left us to machinate while she did the books.

Mike had been charting everything up as we learned it, and now he was staring at the sheets of paper as though expecting them to change into the answer, the way they used to in the G-man movies.

"It appears," said Chester at length, "that we've got a lot more of the information we had when this whole thing started this evening, but we don't appear to have learned anything much except that the Aliens can originate as well as duplicate—which puts them above ninety per cent of the writers I know."

This was not one of Chester's pronouncements that I was about to straight-line for, so I picked up Michael's notes and started looking them over.

"That isn't true," said Michael. "For one thing, we've learned that it isn't confined to our immediate circle, which is something of relief. We also know that it's only been going on for about two days; no reports earlier. And there's also your point about their being able to create without copying."

Chester took his recorder out of his omnipresent briefcase, unscrewed the bowl, and played an experimental trill. "What I'd like to know," he broke off to remark, "is how they got the information on us in the first place."

"Russian submarines," I grumbled, poring over the names and data. It was our stock answer for anything that year.

"Seriously, gentlemen," Chester persisted, "the Aliens had to have some way of observing us in order to make such perfect copies. Nobody was peeking in our windows, and we didn't feel any strange rays or whatever. How did they scan us?"

Michael grumped. "I don't know that it would do us any good to find out. What we—"

"Eureka!" I screamed, cartwheeling spectacularly out of my chair and onto the table.

"Yes?" said Mike equably.

"For once," I said, "I've got an answer to a question."

4

M ichael was skeptical. "What, as Gertrude Stein once said, is the question?"

I nodded toward Chester. "Yours, about how they were watching us. It's only a theory, but it wouldn't be too difficult to check. Looky here."

I ran my finger down the lists of names. "All of these people, with one exception, have vidiphones, legally or otherwise, and vidiphones aren't all that common yet. The camera on the vidip isn't supposed to work when you're not using the phone, but we know how true that is."

"Fascinating," said Chester. "Who, pray, is the exception?"

"That's the most interesting part. The only person who doesn't have one lives in a building that has leased its roof to the phone company for a vidiphone microwave tower that services the whole Lower East Side area."

"Thomas," Chester said ominously.

"Ah, yes, yes. Our late friend with the songs and dances, Mystic Jake."

"Lovely," murmured Chester, closing his eyes in rapture. "Just perfect."

"In that case," said Michael, "that whole bit he went through about chasing himself up Second Avenue was just to throw us off the track."

"Probably," I agreed, "but it's only theory so far. We'll have to check it out."

The two of them stared at me patiently.

"All right, *I'll* have to check it out."

Chester smiled seraphically. "I'll check around at our various abodes and see if there's anything odd about our vidiphones, and we'll see you later at Michael's."

Michael was having a violent argument with himself and seemed to be losing. After several snorts and a grumph, he stood up and scooped the papers together, handing them to Chester. "I'd better go along with Tom," he explained. "He'll need a lookout, and besides, I know more about microwave circuits than he does."

Chester merely nodded and began to play a sedate version of Taps as Mike and I left.

"You don't really have to come along," I offered.

"Don't remind me," said Mike, as we trudged along Bleecker Street in the general direction of Jake's pad. "I feel bad enough as it is."

It was pretty dead along our trail at this hour of the morning. Only a lone bakery truck broke the silence, and even the bums had given up for the night, which was a slight blessing.

We turned down toward Rivington Street. "I just had a thought."

"I'll accept anything at this point," said Mike. "To wit, what?"

"Suppose Mystic Jake is still there—suppose he's asleep?"

Michael shook his head. "Jake wouldn't be there—one of the clubs stays open until six, and he hangs on until the bitter end."

"It was only a thought."

Then we were there. The building had once been a brownstone, but now it was a sort of dirt moldstone. No rat given to nervousness would've stayed in it for a second. The long ground floor hallway was its main entertainment, featuring graffiti in three languages and uncountable perversions. Too, someone had taken pity on the illiterate, for there were several drawings; crude, like those in instructional manuals, but just as functional.

Michael decided to post himself under the stairwell and wait for the high sign from me, which seemed reasonable enough. I went up the stairs and up the stairs and up the stairs for a while, and finally reached the top floor, where Mystic Jake's pad inevitably had to be.

After a pause to acclimatize myself to the thin air, I crept
stealthily toward Jake's door, rather difficult as I was wheezing
like an insane pulmotor.

Locked.

Well, that was the end of that. I'd tried, I had done my best,
but I couldn't go any further. It had been a nice idea, but—

The door swung open. It had been caught on a nail.

It wasn't going to be my day. I moved in and gave the place a
quick general once-over. No Jake, which was something, but not
much of anything else, either. There were moldering stacks of
Variety, Cashbox, and one lone *Crawdaddy* which someone must've
given him out of pity. The place was furnished in early Avenue
A—plastic table, plastic chairs, plastic seatcovers, plastic flowers,
plastic curtains. I knew people who'd furnished better from the
streets—but that was too proletarian for Jake. Well, if he ever
wanted to move he could always melt the whole apartment down
into one big ball.

There wasn't much else of interest. The other suit was hanging
in the closet, two boxes of cereal in the kitchen, a dish of plastic
grapes on top of the vidiphone, dirty laundry in the—

On top of the *vidiphone*?

I ran back to the front room.

It was there, all right, and it seemed to be hooked up and
working. There were some extra wires protruding from the rear
of the thing; they ran behind one of the plastic window curtains
and up out of sight.

Score One for my theory. Mystic Jake had lied to us about not
having a vidip, and he was too status-conscious to have done it
without a good reason. I flicked it on and punched a few buttons
experimentally. The circuits hummed noncomittally for a few
seconds, and then Chester's careworn visage appeared.

Chester scrutinized the screen. "Good Lord! Where are
you?"

"At Mystic Jake's, *naturellement.* He seems to have been
deceiving us about having a vidip, and I wanted to test it."

Drinking this in, Chester looked about the room, as much of
it as he could see on the vidip. "Certainly fits in with the rest of
him," he observed. "Where is the Theodore Bear?"

"Downstairs keeping an eye peeled for Jake. I'm going to take a peek up on the roof, see if there's anything funny with the microwave tower."

"Mmm. Best of luck, T. Waters, and I'll see you both at M. T. Bear's pad." We switched out simultaneously.

Out in the hall it was still quiet, like a sick frog strange noises but nothing that sounded threatening. I could see Mike at the bottom of the stairwell, but he wasn't looking up and I didn't feel like doing anything loud enough to attract his attention.

The door onto the roof fortunately had no lock, and I stepped out into the coolth. It's a lovely feeling to stand on a roof in the dead hour before morning (God, what phrase-turning!), and imagine you're a cat burglar somewhere in Paris. You can only do this facing East or West; if you look south you see the Wall Street skyscrapers, and if you look north you see the huge Con Edison clock and, beyond it, the King Kong exercise Pole—and it breaks the illusion.

I had almost forgotten that in my case it *wasn't* completely illusion; I had broken and entered not ten minutes before. The difference, it was, between objective and poetic truth.

The microwave tower stood at one end of the roof, a squat, thin-legged affair that looked something like a giant spider laden with boxes. The boxlike things were the antennae, and at first glance the tower seemed pretty much like the other ones I'd seen.

On closer examination, however, my best suspicions were confirmed. An odd sort of cable, made of what looked like woven green vines, led from the tower's innards down along the roof and over the edge. A queasy peek confirmed that it went in Jake's window—it was probably attached to the wires I'd seen there before.

This was all very heartwarming, but so far it didn't mean a peep in paradise. It could just be that Jake, like a few of us, had installed an illegal vidip. It was doubtful, since he had once burned out six guitars and a harp by the simple act of turning them on, but it was possible. I would have to get electronics expert Michael up here to take a look. The thought of climbing all those flights of stairs again made me precognitively tired, but there was nothing for it but to get going.

Mike was nowhere to be seen, stairwellwise, when I looked down from Jake's floor, and even more disturbing were the sounds of footsteps and the sight of a hand that seemed to be hopping up the railing a few floors below. Even at that distance I recognized it from the gum-machine diamond ring on its pinky; Mystic Jake was coming home, and what had happened to Superspy?

It *still* wasn't my day; now the door to the roof refused to open. Running tippytoe back down the stairs, I slid into Jake's apartment and closed the door as it had been before, and had a quick reconnaissance.

The footfalls were getting closer now, and the slide-glumph rhythm confirmed that it was indeed Jake.

I knew Mystic Jake well enough to realize that he would've loved to find me here, caught grime-handed. Once, years before, I had used some very underhand tactics to pry his hooks out of a chick singer; Jake had been enraged at the use of his own methods against him, and since then we'd carried on a sporadic war of skirmishing. Of course, without a witness he wouldn't be able to prove anything, and he would know this; but he'd have a weird sort of moral victory and we'd both know it.

The trouble was, there wasn't any place to hide—or was there?

I hadn't noticed it before, but the vidiphone was sitting on top of a wooden crate, angled out from the corner. There might be just enough room. I slid behind the vidip and scrunched down.

The open side of the box was toward me, and there were a lot more wires in it. They were probably live, but as long as I was reasonably careful there wasn't

ZZAP!

5

The leader of the drill formation, I decided, was just not flowing correctly; you'd think that someone on parade at a Staff Officer inspection would have learned Basic Cohesion, but he was spreading all over the place and his edges were very poorly defined.

"Liquid!" I burst out, rotating my central plasm to leave. The other officers were shocked at profanity from someone of my rank, but I was in no mood to notice. They could go achieve fission, for all I cared.

I sank down through the alignment grille-screen and extruded a lead filament into the War Room channel. It would take a while to get there this way, but it was all downhill and I just didn't feel like using the compression tube. I needed time to think.

This whole idea of an invasion, it seemed to me, had nothing to do with our real needs here on Trisk. They never had before, either, when I was just out of the Academy and had hardly mastered geometric forms, but I was young then and looking for glory.

After a few thousand planetfalls, a few million sun-circuits, though, you have to stop and take stock of yourself, and what you want out of life. I had; and I was tired of the whole routine—infiltration, confusion, panic, and victory. What did it get us?

And the beings we won over, what were they? Usually helpless and stupid. I'd one from the Clidge Campaign as a pet, for a while; not only did it cease function in less than fifty circuits, but it kept the same general shape the whole time! A good thing it didn't last longer—it would have driven me mad from boredom.

Here we were, notwithstanding, getting ready to do the whole thing over again. I'd absorbed the reports; the target this time was a Class Nine planet way over in parameter Sann, with one satellite. Not only was it completely out of the way; our geogroup there found a fairly high toxic index in solids, deadflows, and gases.

Pointless.

The War Room was nearly full and I flowed into a central position. The Chairman called the meeting to order.

"We are here to discuss the motion of Solidus Plim," all probes centered on me, "who has suggested we reconsider our planned operations in the Sann para. In view of his high rank and long experience, I propose that we waive the usual procedure and permit him to make a statement of Pattern."

There was a general flash of agreement, and the Chairman indicated I should proceed. Well, may as well start off in an unpopular way; I knew my thoughts weren't going to affect what happened much, in the final analysis. "Chairman Plik, Officers, Coordinators: First of all, I'm not here to make a statement of a Pattern."

They seemed startled, but no one was about to interrupt.

"I'm here to question the Pattern itself. I know, I know, the Pattern has been used since before the oldest of us here had formed his basic unit. I should like to suggest that this is what's wrong with it.

"We are beings of Change. The very base of our existence is mastery over the transience of form and rule—yet for much of our history we have wasted time in acquiring planet after planet. True, we have lost nothing, not even one life, in these wars, but that is to be expected in dealing with ephemeral forms. The point I wish to make is that we have gained nothing for ourselves except information that serves no purpose, and the beings we conquered have become mindless slaves of no use either to us or themselves. My proposal is simple; we simply leave these beings alone, at least until we have studied the Pattern to determine its real value to us."

I had planned to go on, but the hostility was too plain for there to be any point in it. To be against a particular campaign, whatever the reason, would have been bad enough; to question the rightness of the Pattern itself was enough, I knew, to nullify my plea in spite of my position and reputation.

As I had expected, I was requested to withdraw to the Hold chamber while they deliberated. It didn't take long.

The Chairman brought me the news, while behind him the officers interflowed in amused contempt. "We have placed you, Solidus, in a condition of Variance, which as you know means you must undergo an examination for Pattern-flow."

I made no comment; I'd almost expected this—but I didn't expect what followed. "You will leave on the next warp for Sann para, where you will work on the operation. That is all." Before I could reply Chairman Plik had webbed into the exit-grille and departed.

Certainly I had made my stand; now I was going to pay for being so honest.

I took a compression tube up to the surface and rolled out toward the flatlands. It was Quadrine, and my four shadows made a pleasant pattern.

Perhaps it wouldn't be quite so bad; I'd have to keep to the Pattern, of course, if I didn't want to face dissolution, but perhaps I could win against Plik and his bunch of semiforms while using their own rules. It might—

Suddenly I had to stop moving. For some reason my flow had been checked, and I was beginning to solidify along pentagonal axes. The feeling was frightening; had someone contaminated me or was

ZZAP!

6

M uch . . . chance . . . of . . . getting . . . a . . . shock.

Mystic Jake had just come in the door, but with the state my head was in I hardly noticed. He wouldn't see me back here, and maybe when he was distracted I could sneak out by flowing along the baseboard.

By flowing along the baseboard.

Well, practically everyone I knew had been in an Academy For The Bewildered at one time or another, and it had finally come round to my turn. I'd never had a chance to dabble in basketry or finger painting, and it might be fun to let them take out all my springs and wheels and cords to find the one that broke. *Flowing?* Wait a minute. I hadn't just picked that out of the backroads of my memory where it rested ever gentle on my mind. There was something very strange going on here, and somehow I knew that just labeling it as a garden-variety insanity was not going to help any.

Jake was trundling about the apartment making noises I preferred not to analyze, so I occupied myself with looking at the wiring. Though I didn't have Michael's Tom Swiftian capabilities in the electronics field, it was easy to see that this was not a setup for a standard pirate vidiphone. That vinelike cable I'd seen from the roof split into several smaller vines in amidst the tangle, and these in turn were grafted on to vidip wires in a manner that made it look as though they'd grown there.

There was a shuffling sound and a strong smell of cheap hair lotion; Jake was now at the vidiphone, close enough for me to touch if I wanted to, only I didn't want to.

And where the Hell was Michael?

That, as I learned later, was another story—one I had learned as a child, to be exact.

In spite of his earlier misgivings, Mike was rather contented as I ascended to Mystic Jake's pad. He was thinking: *back in the old trade again*.

When the military no longer needs guard dogs, they generally destroy them—the reason being that the dog has been taught to react to the world in a hostile and paranoid way, and can't be readjusted to civilian life. They don't extend this procedure to human beings, however, and the result quite often turned out to be like Michael or me, both alumni of military intelligence organizations. We tended not to accept anything at face value, and had constructed intricate philosophies on this premise. The problem, of course, came with those things which only *had* one value; we'd discard that and be left with nothing, like raccoons washing saltine crackers.

So it was comforting for Michael to apply his reactions to the pattern they were meant for, and he was having a fine time crouched under the stairwell in an attitude of Lurk.

Up to a point.

Only a few minutes had gone by when Mike sensed a sort of change in the atmosphere; there was a closed-in feeling to it, and it was several seconds before Mike realized it was because he *was* closed in. There seemed to be a brown rug hanging behind, him where none had been before. While Mike's head patiently told him to analyze this new phenomenon, his body had gone into a low somersaulting dive, and he felt a little undercurrent of pleasure at the grace with which he rolled out and up to a standing position, facing the rug.

But it wasn't a rug. It was a huge brown bear, and it was gazing at him intently.

Mike found himself running east along Rivington Street toward the river without having any clear memory of leaving Mystic Jake's building. There were clumphing footfalls behind him; the bear was following, but not like any self-respecting ursine.

It was running along on its hind legs in human fashion. Vaguely, as he puffed along, Mike thought he had noticed something else, but now was no time to check—the bear was closing the gap.

Mike was a little out of condition, but apparently so was the bear; as it jogged up alongside he could hear it wheezing, far louder than himself.

The bear definitely had a point to make. With a huge gasp it cried out, *"Christopher?"*

Mike made a dead stop, but the bear wasn't quite so lucky. It went head over heels, did a couple of spectacular cater-cornered revolutions, and stopped, sitting on its rump facing him.

It was a brown bear, all right, but now Mike realized what his mind hadn't registered before; it was a brown *teddy* bear. It was wearing a black jacket far too small for it, and was holding a straw hat in a front paw.

Mike started to say something but the bear shook its head and motioned for a pause. When it had caught its breath, the bear cleared its throat and repeated, "Christopher?" This time there seemed to be a slight imploring note.

It can be very traumatic to have to disappoint an eight-foot-tall teddy bear at first meeting, but there seemed no other way. "Sorry," Mike said shaking his head, "I'm afraid you've mistaken me for someone else. I'm Michael Kurland."

The bear's black-marble eyes got wider and its lower jaw trembled. "Christopher?" it pleaded.

Mike hated scenes. "Honest now, look, I know how it is, but I'm not who you want, I'm not Christopher. I'm sorry, I'm going to have to go now." Mike turned to leave.

"CHRISTOPHER!" wailed the bear, and buried its head in its paws and began to sob uncontrollably.

As if I didn't already have enough problems, Mike thought; a hysterical giant teddy bear. Thomas is never going to accept this one.

And the day was only beginning.

Actually, I would have accepted anything at that moment in preference to being stuck where I was, with aromatic Mystic Jake a bare three feet away. He was punching in what seemed like an endless stream of digits, far too many for any regular call.

Then—there might've been something visible on the screen but I couldn't see it—then a voice rapped out in metallic tones: "Activate the extruder, Lord Sheba!" *Lord Sheba?*

This I could see, by squinting through a crack in the box. Jake set a small metal tube down on the floor, and slid a translucent ring of some material down over the cylinder. Immediately it began to pulse softly, and then from the open top what looked like rainbow-colored mud began to flow out on to the floor. There was far more of the stuff than the tube could possibly have contained, and a good-sized blob of it had appeared in a few seconds. Then, just as suddenly, the flow stopped and the tube fell silent.

Abrupdy the blob extended itself upward, and then it wasn't a blob any longer.

It was me.

7

I was beside myself.

Well, not quite, but I could have reached out from my hiding place and touched me without any difficulty. I thought of Burns' line about the "gift the good Lord gie us, to see oursels' as others see us."

It was a reasonably safe bet that any Lord you cared to name would have denied any part in what I was seeing now, but I could gie a damn about the theology; looking at the surrogate me and realizing that it was what I looked like to others was a somewhat harrowing experience. At first the fake, which I shall designate as Null-T, looked somehow wrong, but then I realized it was because all my life I'd been seeing a mirror image of myself instead of my true appearance. It was a strange sort of thing to try to accept a new orientation after all this time.

Null-T and Mystic Jake were talking; Null-T, with what seemed like a psychic ventriloquism, using my voice, and Jake giving with his standard oleaginous drone. I didn't have to strain to hear, not a bit.

"How proceeds the patterning, Lord Sheba?" asked Null-T.

"Things is really movin' beautiful." Didn't sound like a Lord but it certainly sounded like Jake. "All sorts a people really uptight, man. Lissen, whenayou gonna drop with this local crap and do the big thing, man? I mean, y'know, it's workin' great so far, man, why don't y'just freak out the whole world and get yer thing going here, huh, man? Huh?"

I was impressed with Null-T's ability to communicate with someone who had Mystic Jake's speech patterns; a lot of us had been trying for years, with no luck at all.

"Such a procedure as you suggest, Lord Sheba, is as you very well know quite impossible. We must adhere to the Pattern until it indicates the proper stage has been reached."

"Y'don't wanna do it, huh, man?" Jake had a direct mind—at least in some senses.

"At present it is not of the Pattern." The Alien smiled, a difficult thing to try doing with my face. "Be patient, Lord Sheba. The time will come, and you will be rewarded as befits you."

There was a curious edge to my—that is, to Null-T's—voice, but Jake didn't seem to notice it. He had only managed to apprehend the essential fact that he wasn't going to get the jackpot just yet.

"Yeah, well, awright," he said, like an adolescent Jack The Ripper being told he couldn't use the butcher knife tonight. "Whadda we do now, then, huh?"

"You continue with your surveillance of the operation," answered Null-T. "I trust you have encountered no areas of flowcheck—ah, pardon me—no problems thus far?"

Mystic Jake laughed, a sound like a baby being strangled. Incompetently.

"Naw, man. There was only those three I tole you about, Anderson, Kurland, and Waters, the guy you're doin' now, but I conned them real easy. They think it's happenin' to me, too, the imitation thing, so that's not no problem. Man, they don't really know who they're dealin' with, how smart I really am."

"That is quite probable," said Null-T after a pause, but the nuance went through Jake like milk of magnesia. "We must proceed now. Continue with your duties as before, Lord Sheba." This was a dismissal, but the tone of voice made it unsubtle enough for Jake to catch the general idea.

"Yeah, uh, er . . ." Mystic Jake departed along a daisy chain of interjections. Null-T sighed, and seemed to run slightly like an overheated wax statue of me, but then he pulled himself together. He picked up the tube and set the ring to one side.

Null-T pressed the tube in an odd way and a small globe of light appeared at the top.

"Private diary entry 3-A: I'm proceeding with the operation and so far it looks like a typical Pattern. The Instigator we've picked is just barely adequate, but he'll serve his purpose until Full Pattern and Total Web goes into effect, now scheduled for five Earth days. Solidus Plim arrived Shipside and is now in Pattern. So far he's adhering, but I continue to doubt the advisability of bringing him here; if he becomes unstable it could create problems. Entry closes."

The ball of light winked out and Null-T tossed the cylinder onto the couch. He looked around the room abstractedly, and then, after studying himself briefly in Jake's grimy mirror, departed. I was alone with my thoughts, and they weren't very good company.

Question time, Waters.

Q: Why did the Alien speak in English?

A: Probably because he was in human form and couldn't use his own kind of speech.

Q: Passable. What about that stuff about "Full Pattern and Web"?

A: It sounds suspiciously like they're planning to do this duplicating worldwide in less than a week.

Q: Alarmist. Why would they do that?

A: I suppose to create mass confusion and . . .

(arpeggio from unseen pianist)

. . . take over the world.

Q: What, again?

A: Listen, none of this was my idea. Quit picking on me.

Q: And why, may I ask, when

> *aliens*
> *extraterrestrials*
> *bug-eyed monsters*
> *little green men*
> *intellects,*
> *vast, cool, and unsympathetic*
> *or other such, decide to invade do they*

always pick on the Unholy Three, i.e., Anderson, Kurland, and Waters?

A: (defensively) I don't know. Maybe we have something in common.

(CURTAIN. Audience rises, picking up hats and coats, and murmurs puzzledly.)

All of this did not take long, because when I argue with myself I always have the uncomfortable knowledge that I'm going to lose; I therefore do it fast to get it over with.

Being careful not to touch that stray wire again (I'd *certainly* have to check with Mike about *that*), I squoze back out of my hiding place. My replica was still very audibly galumphing down the stairs and my proper course of action was to follow, but first I had to persuade my blood that I was still alive and that it should get moving again.

Null-T was nearly a block away by the time I left the building, and I decided to maintain the distance.

He was headed in a general way toward Mike's apartment, to do, I wondered, what?

It was an interesting exercise. Since Null-T was using my vocabulary and speech patterns, as well as my appearance, I could logically assume that such thought processes as he needed to deal with human-type problems would be pretty much mine. One such problem, I reasoned, would be being tailed.

They'd given us a course, way back in the dear dead days of Military Intelligence, on Methods of Surveillance, and a lot of the training had stuck with me. I was fairly competent in the better methods of tailing, but more importantly, I knew what I—and therefore Null-T—would be watching for, what would make me suspicious.

This rather baroque theory, to my surprise, worked fine in practice; I had no trouble keeping Null-T under observation all the way to the Lower Depths—Mike's street.

It was possible I might lose the *fake* me now, because I had to drop the tail long enough to call Chester from one of the few vidiphone cubiques that hadn't been vandalized.

"Ah, Thomas. Good evening. Pray, what has been the delay?" Chester was pleasant, wide awake and alert; I wondered what he was on.

"Listen, I'm a couple of blocks up the street and I should be there very shortly—*very* very shortly, but the *first me that comes in won't be me. It'll be one of our friendly Aliens.*"

"Come again?" Maybe Chester wasn't so awake after all.

"At Mystic Jake's. I was messing around after I called you when both Jake and an Alien came in—by different ways. The whatever, something like intelligent silly putty, sort of reared up, and then it was me, right down to the clothes."

"*Those* clothes?"

"Chester, this is not the time to—"

"Wait a second," said Chester. "If there is a fake you, how do I know whether it's you or—"

Bam.

Bam.

Bam.

"—what is pounding at the door in your ingratiating way?"

"A good point," I agreed, "but I have an idea. Just keep it talking until I get there. Leave the door ajar and await developments."

"Mmff." The screen went dark. That had been Chester's I-don't-like-it-but-what-the-hell grunt. This was where things would get interesting.

Promises, promises.

A few minutes later I slipped into the hall of Mike's pad. The stentorian sounds of conversation told me that Null-T was haggling over how many time-breaks were forked in using the Coin Oracle for the *I Ching*. I began to wonder about Null-T's abilities; I was *sure* I could have done better.

Chester saw me as I swung round the arch into the living room, but Null-T wasn't quite as quick; his head had only started to turn when I brought the Pepsi bottle (family size) down on his head. Chester eyed me suspiciously.

"If you're you, that wasn't a very *you* sort of thing to do," he said.

I was about to reply when Null-T eliminated the need for it. What had been my sprawled-out form (and it gave me a creepy goosefleshy sort of feeling to look at it) suddenly began to change. In less than five seconds it was a perfect scale model of a World War I biplane, propeller turning. It zipped across the floor, leaving it and climbing steeply after a five-foot run. It circled the room once, fired a short burst from its forward machine gun that came nowhere near us, and then did a beautiful Immelmann into the hallway and out through the still-open door.

"Spectacular," I conceded, wondering what the local population would make of this.

"Flashy," Chester demurred, "but it does solve what we may refer to as your identity crisis, unless you have unplumbed depths as a warlock."

I sat down and lit something friendly. "There is one overwhelming impression I get from what's been happening since all this started—one pattern that seems to run like an unbreakable thread through everything."

"And what's that?" Chester was being obliging.

"We don't seem to be getting anywhere. It's like fighting in a fog."

Chester didn't think so. "We've found out a number of things about them, aside from the fact of their existence, and we have the edge in that they don't know just how much we've learned. Also, we've both seen them change shape and faced duplicates of ourselves."

"Mmm. I suppose you've got a thought there—the only one of us left to go through that rather chastening experience is Mike."

"Ah, yes." Chester gazed dreamily up at where there would have been sky if there hadn't been building. "And where *is* Michael?"

8

ike still had problems.

A problem, to be exact; an eight-foot-tall, brown-furred, marble-eyed, theoretically cuddly problem.

It was quite light now, though there were blessedly few people on the streets. Mike headed back toward Mystic Jake's, afraid that something might have happened during his unscheduled excursion. Had we all but known, as the saying goes. The bear followed along, a respectful three paces to the rear; every so often it murmured "Christopher?" under its peppermint breath, but otherwise it was a model of decorum.

At the foot of the almost endless stairs to Mystic Jake's, Mike stopped abruptly and turned to face the bear, who instantly halted and looked back at him with nervous uncertainty.

"Now look," said Mike in his most reasonable voice, which is not very, "this is getting ridiculous. I can't have a bear following me around, particularly a teddy bear. People would say I'm flaunting my image. You'll just have to find somebody else to follow."

The bear was unmoved. *"Christopher,"* it said, enunciating the syllables carefully as though it were trying to teach Mike how to say it.

"All right," said Mike, "I tried. I have to go upstairs here but I'll be right back down," he lied. Suddenly something occurred to him. "Listen. If you're going to hang around, why don't you make a hat like this"—sketching on the wall with his omnipresent marker styl—"and pants like this. At least it'll keep you out of trouble." Mike had no idea where the bear would get the stuff, but if it was what he thought it would have no problem—and if people spotted the bear wandering about (he wasn't that easy to overlook), they were less likely to panic.

The bear was still watching Mike doubtfully when he lost sight of it around an angle of the stairwell. Well, at least that was one problem out of the way.

Mike was being optimistic.

The apartment was, of course, empty, and after one look at the innards of the vidiphone Mike became extremely doubtful about using it. Better to call from an outside booth in any case, because during the day Mystic Jake's schedule was erratic and highly unpredictable.

By this time Mike was definitely in an unbearable mood; people weren't where they should be, and this giant teddy bear was peripatetically ubiquitous (ah!).

There was always, of course, the roof, and Mike did his Class 4-A Skulk across several tenemental conjoinings before he found an open roof door. The sun was above the horizon, as nearly as he could tell from the faint luminosity in the eastern haze: the day would be warm and muggy, followed by Tugy, Weggy, Thurgy, and Frigy.

Ignoring the puzzling and sometimes ominous scents that wafted out from the various apartments, Mike made his way down to the ground floor and out the door.

"Christopher," said the bear somewhat sternly.

It wasn't going to be as simple as Mike had hoped. The bear waited patiently outside the cubique while Mike tried to reach us at his apartment, unsuccessfully because we'd gone out in search of food. On the Lower East Side this can be an all-day project if you don't want your breakfast to contain unadvertised or charged-for fauna. Mike's own go-away-don't-bother-me message flashed on, and he watched through it fully twice before deciding that he really meant what he was saying to himself.

The bear followed at its customary three paces as Michael headed west toward MacDougal Street. A few people, notably cops, seemed somewhat put out by this spectacle, but calls to HQ Central only confirmed their suspicions that nothing in the Code prohibited being followed by a bear, be it *ursus horriblis* or *ursus theodorus.* Other onlookers were positively charmed by the whole thing, and by the time Mike reached the MacDougal-Bleecker nexus he was the titular head of a parade, consisting of children, hippies, winos, optional psychos, photographers, revolutionaries, and unclassifiables. It was a very impressive demonstration, and if Michael could only have figured out of what he would have been much happier.

What to Mike's wondering eyes should have appeared *did,* in the form of Amy Muscar, arm-in-arm with Frederick, Mike's younger brother. Frederick looked exactly like a Frederick, only more so; mustache segueing into muttonchops and brushed-back wavy hair behind a face that could only be described as incipient Lafayette Escadrille. The rest of his outfit reinforced the image; no one else was wearing silk mufflers at this time of the year.

"You have a bear," Frederick pointed out to Mike politely.

"What about it?" Mike was being defensive.

"It's a teddy bear," continued Frederick in the same careful tone; he wasn't completely sure that the furry apparition behind Mike couldn't be a problem of his own.

Amy decided to be helpful. "You're auditioning for the part of Antigonus in *The Winter's Tale*"? she suggested hopefully.

The crowd was beginning to disperse. The teddy bear was just standing there, after all, and the novelty had worn off. Even God couldn't hold a New York crowd very long, unless he did something spectacular like walk across the Hudson . . . not even that; the old trader's river was so full of garbage that walking across it wouldn't be a strain on the most confirmed atheist.

"I don't *have* a bear," said Mike. "Slavery has been abolished. Anyway, he's just been following me around because he thinks I'm somebody named Christopher." The bear's expression perked up at this and Mike shot it an annoyed glance. "I can't convince it to leave me alone and go pick on somebody else."

"You haven't by any chance set a forest fire?" inquired Amy.

Mike shook his head. "No, no, the clothes are my idea. If he was still wearing that idiot straw hat and jacket I'd really be in trouble." Frederick and Amy looked at Mike strangely but he didn't explain.

The boy-girl pair, after a pause, smiled uncertainly and wandered off. The spy-teddy bear duo silently watched them depart, Mike with a casually vague horniness thinking of Amy's fair white body, and the bear thinking, presumably, *Christopher.*

Noting with mild surprise that the Pentalpha was open this early in the day, Mike sauntered in with his cuddly shadow close behind. Weinie, the manager, was at the cash register counting the previous night's receipts, and he glanced up as Mike and the bear plopped down at a table back in the shadows near the Kallikak box. "Hi, Mike," he said pleasantly, and indicated the bear with a nod. "Who's your friend?" Weinie had been in the Village an awfully long time.

"He's no friend of mine," grumped Mike. The bear stared down at the table morosely and murmured almost inaudibly, *"Christopher."* Someone able to read the expression on the teddy bear's face would have interpreted it: *I know he's really Christopher, and it's cruel of him not to admit it.* Mike, however, no longer tried to read expressions! the last time he'd tried it was with an Edsel and he wasn't able to unpucker for a week.

Mike was still sitting there some time later, when Chester and I appeared. He looked at us expectantly as we sat down, and when by mutual telepathic agreement neither Chester nor I would break the silence, Mike finally said, "All right. Go ahead, say it. You particularly, Chester, since you nicknamed me, this should be your finest hour."

"?" said Chester.

"Don't be cutesy," grumbled Mike, staring at the table. "Go ahead, ask me about the bear."

"Que-est que c'est bear?" inquired Chester.

Mike looked around wildly, and discovered that his cuddly curse had indeed departed, so silently and unobtrusively that Mike had no idea how long it had been gone.

"It *would* be nice," I said finally, "if you'd tell us what's been going on."

Michael filled us in on his ursine adventures, and then in story and song Chester and I gave him a rundown on the events of the night. Mike didn't really seem interested until I described what had been Null-T's unorthodox departure.

"A *biplane,* you say?" He brightened. "Did you happen to get a look at the wing markings?"

"Forget it, Michael," I said. "I know it's one of your consuming interests in life but I don't really think it's apposite to the problem at hand. We've got to stop messing around and formulate some sort of plan of action."

"Well . . ."

For the next couple of hours we were in earnest discussion. It would have been beautiful if we'd been talking about the forthcoming invasion, but we somehow got sidetracked into a discussion of sadism in science fiction, as exemplified in Andy Blake's new series *Lash Cordon, Worldbeater.* This afforded us a few philosophical laughs which not even the knowledge that Blake was getting rich from it could dim—but thinking about the writing didn't help our syntax any.

Time had, to coin a phrase, flown, and Weinie came over to remind me that it was time for my evening set. Mike and Chester agreed to hang around until I was finished, and I went into the back room to set my props. The cockroach was still sitting on the solitary chair, and now it had an honor guard of two huge waterbugs. I decided not to use the chair, and as I set up the gimmicks the antennae of the three semaphored an immense disdain.

It was a nice crowd, no rowdies, and the questions were the usual type:

Q: I'm troubled at home, what's good for mice?

A: Cheese is the best thing I can think of . . .

About thirty such gems and I was finished; back at the table, Mike and Chester congratulated me on getting through the entire routine without having to use one original line.

Now where were we? Ah, yes, the invasion; we had to formulate some plan of action. Right. Yes . . .

But not, as it happened, quite yet.

9

At first glance, we weren't quite sure that the guy who had suddenly appeared at our table out of the candle-smoke haze wasn't an Alien invader himself.

He was certainly shapeless enough. Neither he nor his clothes had a sharp edge between them; there were rolls of slightly dirty cuff, soft hollow bulges, and bagginesses in places they had no right to be—and his face was furnished the same way, with round, soft features. You could only have drawn him with a crayon.

Having misspent several years in coffee houses, we were used to the various types other than customers who would wander in. There were, first of all, the panhandlers: Standard, Alcoholic, Speed Freak, and Psychotic.

Then there were the tourists, who also came in various categories: Wary Intruder, Quaintness Spotter, Weirdo Observer, and Know-Your-Enemy Old Guard.

Another genus were the pamphleteers: Religious, Political, and Commercial.

Finally there were the dealers, who had dropped considerably in prestige and community standing when most mind drugs became legal. Now they only had a few things to offer that couldn't be got cheaper elsewhere: Moon-Snuff, Lobotomycin, Psytrol, and, occasionally, Reality Pills. Whenever one of these last was offered for sale Chester went home to check his supply, counting it two or three times; there were just so many Reality Pills left, and Chester had spent his maturing years in a pharmacologically protective atmosphere.

Studying this latest, we all placed Shapeless instantly into the Pamphleteer category; we were able to do this with unerring accuracy through long experience, incisive reasoning, and by noting that he was clutching a huge bundle of pamphlets to his chest. He looked down at us somewhat anxiously.

"Have you found him?" he cried.

"No," I replied, equably enough, "have you lost him?"

Shapeless didn't seem at all satisfied with this answer. "I mean HIM!" he elaborated.

"Yeah, Him," Michael chimed in as though ashamed of my obtuseness.

"Oh, yes, Him." I considered.

"Yeah," Shapeless seemed pleased, "yeah, Him."

"Hymn?" Chester suggested experimentally, but Shapeless paid him no heed. Heed was very tight that year.

"No," I decided.

"NO?" Shapeless glared at me. "No, what?"

"No, I haven't found him."

Shapeless was suspicious. "Honest," I added, but it failed to convince him. He studied me carefully, as though certain that I really had found *him* but didn't want to give *him* back. Had I concealed *him* about my person? Unintentionally? I was getting worried.

Shapeless gave us all a stern look of disapproval and then, flicking out with Vegas-dealer skill three pamphlets, churned away in the general direction of the door.

The pamphlet retailed the experiences of one Perry Diogenes. Mr. Diogenes, it appeared, had been born into a poor family in the little mining town of Orbal, Pennsylvania. A hero in the classic Alger mold, he started working in the mines when he was eight. By dint of ambition and a not-too-keen moral sense he had attained ownership of the local coal company while still in his twenties, and in a few years more the entire county, give or take a few clay-eaters. His mother, it must be explained, had always been racked by strangely indefinite pains, and now Mr. Diogenes sent her to a clinic in Switzerland where continuous attention made life bearable for her.

Mr. Diogenes had a younger brother, whose greatest desire had always been to become a painter; Mr. Diogenes saw to it that the young man was well fed and clothed, and a studio in New

York was provided for him, and the younger brother's instructors agreed that his work showed considerable promise.

But Mr. Diogenes was not yet done: he gave the town of Orbal a new hospital and school, had the best of staffs and equipment installed in each, and supported both institutions with his own continuous donations.

Then—Mr. Diogenes found God.

It was not completely clear how this happened, for God was not overly popular in that section of Pennsylvania. Mr. Diogenes himself, writing in the pamphlet, confesses to not being sure how it all came about—mysterious ways and all that—but he thinks it all began when he was in New York on a business trip and was handed a small pamphlet by someone in a restaurant.

Mr. Diogenes tells us that he now saw the error of his ways; that in the pursuit of material success he had neglected the most important of experiences, which he terms "giving his all for the Almighty."

Mr. Diogenes made up for lost time. He liquidated his holdings, including the school and hospital, to a realty company, and sent the money thus realized to an investment corporation— the profits to be used to further the Word, or, if there was enough, possibly even two Words. A clerk at the investment firm absconded with the money and flew to Argentina, where, he had heard, the National Socialists were readying another bid for return to power. The clerk contributed the money to the Bund Fund, and the National Socialists decided to have a party, in the course of which some sourpuss malcontent tossed a grenade into their ammunition dump. The Fourth Reich rose.

It didn't settle back to Earth for a couple of weeks.

Meanwhile, Mr. Diogenes, observing these evil effects of money, was glad he was now destitute. He was tired and weak, of course—the clinic in Switzerland had thrown his mother out for nonpayment of bills, and her coughing and crying kept Mr. Diogenes awake most of the night. It must be said in all fairness that she was crying only partly because of the pain, for she was a courageous woman and Mr. Diogenes had exhorted her not to Lose Faith. For the most part she was crying because, having been dropped out of art school, Mr. Diogenes' younger brother had ended it all by diving head first into the *Times* presses.

The pamphlet closed on an upbeat note, explaining that after Mr. Diogenes had been unable to find work in the collapsing town of Orbal, he moved to New York City, and was now a happy man in the service of the Lord.

He was employed, it said, by an evangelical association, and his job was distributing pamphlets . . .

"Now about that plan," Chester said presently, after we had finished reading the pamphlets and had sat there staring at each other for a while in dreamy horror.

"I'll concede on this one," I said. "Besides, Michael is our warfare expert."

Mike accepted the statement as only his due. In tutorial tones he began: "The theorist Von Clausewitz states that the first principle of war is to obtain a secure base."

Chester was doubtful. "Did Von Clausewitz ever live in the East Village?"

"If you keep interrupting me," he said with only a .5 glower, "I won't be able to work this thing out. I was about to say that, for several reasons, standard principles don't apply here; we just don't have enough to go on. It does seem, however, that the vidip in Mystic Jake's pad is their bottleneck, and that makes it our logical attack point." Mike yawned.

"What's the matter with you?" I asked.

"Nothing. I've just been awake since yesterday, I've been hounded by a bear—that doesn't sound right—and I've had to watch you perform. Doesn't that give me a right to be a little bit tired?"

"Nope," I said, "not until we get this thing taken care of once and for all. For a superhero, Michael, you certainly don't take any pains to keep up your image."

"Gnurph. I take it we are now off to Mystic Jake's."

"Keerect," I affirmed, "and to disassemble the vidip. If Mystic Jake is still there, we might be well advised to do the same with him."

We trundled out into the gaudy Village darkness, with Chester doing a brief rendition of the Colonel Bogey March on his tiny silver LectroCorder. Breaking off the tune just at the beginning of the best part, he said, "It appears to me that we might have a problem there. How would we know that it's the real Jake and not one of our protean pals?"

"Whatever Mystic Jake's talents are, I'm damn sure he can't turn into a model biplane when somebody starts bopping him with what is classically referred to as a Blunt Instrument. We will just have to take our chances on that score, and Learn By Doing."

A pair of girls walked by, dressed in fishnets that some cunning soul had told them were dresses, and there was a ten-second blank period until they were out of sight. Then Mike said, in a definite and judicial tone, "Yass, yass, no doubt of it, we must make the world safe for such helpless young things."

"Snarf snarf snarf," said Chester and I.

We stopped at the Cafe Nobody to check on arrivals and departures, and discovered that Mystic Jake had been seen about not long before, which meant we had a good chance of not having to bother with him—if what they'd seen was in fact him.

We continued east, and once past Broadway encountered few people we knew; it was the prime part of the evening for socializing and making the rounds of the coffee houses, if you weren't working in them anyway.

Chester was grumbling because of all the walking we'd been doing. Not too long before it wouldn't have been necessary, because Chester had become the proud owner, by default, of the Tripsmobile, an early-model ground-effect machine that his rock group had used for transportation, as well as other things both unprintable and indescribable. It had happened that, on a return trip from the Coast not too long after the Time-Bubble business, the three of us had chanced to arrive in Hershey, Pennsylvania, one Sunday morn, and it seemed like a good idea to go see the candy plant. The fence was no problem for the supercharger on the Tripsmobile, and in we went. Mike was having a little trouble with the controls, but it didn't seem serious, and we noticed just then that the doors to the big vat rooms were open . . .

I'm not going to go into the gory details, but I'm glad I can swim and have a taste for chocolate.

We swung into the current of people moving along Orchard Street, past sidewalk racks and tables displaying everything conceivable and otherwise and vendors anxious to make that big final sale of the evening. The flow carried us to Rivington and we swirled out in a little eddy of humanity; another block and a half and we were back at Mystic Jake's building.

"My, my," said Chester as we climbed the stairs, "you mean to say that if I become a real promoter and business manager for rock-and-rollies that I can live in such posh elegance as this?"

"You scoff," I said, "but this is nice, relatively speaking. Wait till you see the apartment."

"Do I have any choice?" Chester puffed.

This time, interestingly, Jake's door was locked, but it yielded to my tender ministrations after a few moments. We walked in, and after a look round Chester conceded my aesthetic analysis. Mike, meanwhile had already set to work at the vidip, and now he called us over. A pile of wires from behind the device were now in his lap, looking like plastic spaghetti, and he was holding up two strands peeled from one of the cables.

"Hold these for a second," he said, and for some reason Chester and I complied. Mike started cutting through another wire when I remembered something.

"Mike," I began, "don't you think we

ZZAP!

10

We were without form, and void. It was certainly depressing.

11

We had form again, but I for one wasn't so sure it was that much of an improvement.

I was lying on a hillside, in the middle of a huge patch of ivy vines, and every bone in my body ached as though I had been exercising since before a chunk of while. Painfully I got up and took a good look around.

It was a hillside, all right, at the foothills of a mountain range I was positive didn't exist in the United States. A winding dirt road led down along the valley before us, and a few miles distant a village was dimly visible.

Mike and Chester were on their feet now, and we all surveyed the view. "Boss vista," I offered.

"Scenic, if a bit too quaint to be completely credible," said Chester. "Any idea where we *are*?"

Mike frowned at the scenery for a while like an unhappy director. "Eastern Europe," he finally stated. "Bulgaria, or thereabouts."

This seemed as likely as anything. "How do you suppose we got here?" asked Chester.

"Well," I theorized, "that vidiphone in Jake's pad is some sort of transporter for the Aliens. We probably shorted the damn thing and got warped here through some sort of hyperspace."

"If that's true," said Chester, "we're damn lucky it happened to warp us here instead of someplace where they breathe methane and drink ammonia."

Mike started hopping down through the tangle of vines toward the road. "One sure thing," he said, "we're not going to get back that way. We'd better head for that town."

We started bounding down the hill toward the rutted highway, like psychedelic jack rabbits. It was a respectable distance, and by the time we'd reached the bottom we were pretty much out of bounds, not to mention out of breath. We stopped for a fresh supply of air.

Suddenly there was an outlandish creaking clatter in the distance and something rounded the bend at the end of the valley and headed along the road in our general direction. As it came closer we gradually recognized it; a stagecoach-carriage, drawn by four horses. With a terrible din and a crack of the coachman's whip it carreened past us, but before it was lost in a cloud of dust we had seen the legend painted in gilt on the black door:

TRANSYLVANIAN OVERLAND LINES

"Ah, hmm," said Chester, "that certainly solves the problem of *where* we are, but it raises a rather more important question— i.e., *when* are we?"

"If that coach is indicative of the transportation in general, not much later than Nineteen-Ten, and probably near a decade earlier."

Mike was still looking down the road at the now-invisible coach. "Transylvania," he crooned. "Castles. Vampires. Things that go bump in the night."

I wasn't too impressed; the last of those I'd had in every Village pad I'd ever known. Besides, I was bothered, and it wasn't just from being slipped sidewise in time and space; that had happened to me during the Time Bubble thing and I'd ended up in Ogallala, Nebraska—after Ogallala nothing along this line could really bother me. No, it was just a sense of something not fitting correctly; I had the feeling that I was holding a number of different pieces to a jigsaw puzzle, pieces that just didn't quite fit together, and if I could just jiggle them in my mind the right way . . .

We didn't talk much on the way into town, each of us having his own weird little mental circuses. When we reached the fountain in the town square we sank down gratefully and washed our faces in the lovely cool water, somewhat tireder than we had expected to be.

When we finally stood up and looked around, we'd collected a respectable crowd of townspeople, all staring at us curiously. At first I thought it was because of the way we were dressed—I, for example, in neon paisley shirt, op-art levis and ancient calf-length brown boots, and I was the conservative one—but then I noticed that several of them were dressed even more colorfully than Chester, in brilliant gypsy-like costumes.

No, it was probably just because we were newcomers; I could see the black coach that had passed us earlier parked beside a tavern on the other side of the square, and there was a gaggle of locals surrounding it as well.

I motioned to Mike and Chester. "If there are other strangers just in, we'll probably be able to find out a bit more about what's going on than we can from the indigenosia." Nodding and smiling our way through the crowd, we ducked under the low sill of the doorway and into the tavern.

After the brightness of the square it took a moment for my eyes to adjust, and then things came into clear view. There were only two people here, aside from the huge bartender, and they had turned from their seats at the window to look at us.

I recognized them both, and a glance at Mike and Chester told me they knew them too.

One was a sharp-featured man, with a hawklike nose and grey eyes beneath a high forehead; he appeared tall but wiry, and was puffing on a large calabash pipe. His friend was shorter, thickset, with a mustache. Beside him was a black medical bag.

We were looking at the Great Detective himself, and his faithful friend, physician, and chronicler. The pair looked exactly as I had always known they would look.

"Oh, wow," breathed Mike.

"Charming, just charming," affirmed Chester.

"So they still live for all that love them well . . . ," I quoted from Vincent Starret. "Well, my chaps, if anybody can help us out of our present situation, he can."

The tall man stood and gestured to us. "Pray join us, gentlemen, and have some refreshment, which you must sorely need after your wearisome journey." The bartender brought up some extra chairs and we sat down after shaking hands all round.

The tall one introduced himself. "My name is Altamont," he smiled, "and this is my good friend Dr.—Hudson. Whom do we have the pleasure of meeting?"

We all gave our real names, which was more than I suspected Altamont was doing. "From the United States," I added.

"A wonderful country," said Altamont. "I was there as a young man, with a theatrical troupe. America is the promise of a better future."

I let that pass, because the word *future* had set me a bit on edge; there was a question I was going to have to ask, and it would sound strange no matter how I phrased it. I plunged in.

"Mr.—ah—Altamont, my friends and I have a rather curious little problem. We've been traveling for several days, and we seem to have lost track of the calendar. Might I trouble you for the exact date?"

Altamont regarded me strangely for a moment. "It is Saturday, April 30th, 1904," he said finally, and consulting his watch, added, "4:15 p.m."

Dr. Hudson gave a gruff laugh. "My word, Altamont, of course they're going to know the year—unless the sun has baked their senses out of them." We all chortled at this excellent point except Altamont. "Of course," he said in an emotionless tone.

Mike decided to change the subject. "Uh—this doesn't seem like a place that gets many tourists. What on Earth brings you here?"

"A question *I* might well ask," said Altamont. "But since you inquire, I shall answer you; first, however, I must have your oath not to discuss what I shall reveal with any others."

We all swore. Altamont waited pointedly until the bartender had retreated to the far end of the room and then began to speak. "My reason for explaining our mission here to total strangers such as yourselves is a simple one; the Doctor and I may need assistance, and strangers to Transylvania and these Carpathian Mountains are the only ones we dare trust." He paused and lit his pipe.

"I have been retained by the government to investigate a local disturbance that seems to have baffled their own constabulary. In the mountains not two hours' coach ride from here is an ancient castle, supposedly deserted for centuries, that appears to be the starting point of the problem. This problem is that the people of the area are convinced that they are under the scourge of a vampire, and that the loathsome thing has its lair in the crypts of Castle Dracula."

Mike, Chester, and I looked at each other, and Chester muttered, "Ever get the feeling that someone's been tampering with your mythologies?"

"Incredible, of course," said Altamont, who seemed not to have noticed our reaction, "that people would still believe in such things in this modem age, but this is a backward land where many still live as they did centuries ago."

Aside from our basic cosmogonal worries, there was an unpleasant question implied in the early part of what Altamont had said. Trust Mike to verbalize it. "How would we be able to help you?"

Altamont pressed his fingertips together and studied them judiciously. "For my own part, and I believe Dr. Hudson echoes my thoughts on this, I do not hold with this medieval notion of vampires. It offends reason, as strongly here as it did years ago in Sussex. At best, this personage known as Count Dracula is for some reason perpetrating a fraud on the populace; at worst, he is a criminal lunatic. In either case it is probable that he has helpers who assist him either through greed or fear, and they may prove troublesome for just Dr. Hudson and me."

Altamont paused and looked up at us. "I am empowered by the government to employ as I require, and I am certain that you would find having negotiable funds helpful."

Subtle but beautiful. If I'd had doubts before about who he was they were gone now. Altamont added, "It is also possible that I can assist you to some degree with your own problems."

Mike tried a bluff line. "What problems do we have?"

Altamont smiled slightly and indicated Dr. Hudson, who was peering out into the haze of dusk. "What man is free of problems?" he said lightly. "We will have time to discuss the situation properly."

He wasn't giving away a thing, but he certainly seemed to have the edge; it would be interesting to see just how much he did know; but that, as he had hinted, would have to wait.

The three of us had a brief council and decided to accept Altamont's job offer; not that we had many alternatives. He was pleased at our decision and ordered an elaborate dinner for us all. The food was good enough, although I couldn't identify a couple of the items, but I was used to that from eating in coffeehouses and it didn't bother me.

Chester and Altamont pretty much divided up the dinner-table conversation between them, and Anderson sat enthralled when Altamont described the performances of Sarasate and Mme. Norman-Neruda. After the meal Altamont got out his violin, and with Chester playing his minicorder we were treated to a classical duet.

During this latterly bit Mike grew more fidgety. He wasn't the type to sacrifice action for aesthetics, and it didn't matter that at this point we had no idea of what action to take. Something had to be done, that was all.

I jockeyed my chair around near Mike's window bench so we could whisper without interrupting the *musicale*. "April 30th, 1904?" I inquired sweetly.

Michael grunted noncommittally in Cyrillic.

"I thought that Time Bubble business was all over with," I said accusingly.

"It is," insisted Mike. "You know that was stopped as well as I do."

"Then what are we doing here, and more importantly, *now*?"

Michael shrugged like a bear with an itch. "The sixty-four dollar question." He was always dating himself that way. "What *I'd* like to know is what those Aliens are doing."

"Relax. They won't be invading for three-quarters of a century." This was another view of the situation but it didn't seem to comfort Mike.

It was high evening by the time we were on our way, in the same black overland coach, which Altamont explained had been provided by his clients. He suggested to Dr. Hudson that he ride with the driver to direct him, and after the burly physician had clambered up to the high seat the coachman flicked his whip above the leader harness and we were off, heading up into the mountains.

The four of us inside the carriage stared at each other for a while. Altamont had lit his calabash again—it was filled with a particularly vile variety of the cheapest shag—and studied us one by one for some time before he finally spoke.

"I am afraid I may not have been completely honest with you gentlemen when I suggested I could help you; indeed, now that I have confirmed my earlier surmise I am not sure that *any* powers that be in this world could relieve your plight."

"Oh?" said Mike, still playing it close to the chest. "And what was your earlier surmise?"

Altamont hesitated only the merest fraction before speaking. "You are strangers here in time as well as space," he stated positively. "Not merely a leap into the past, for you are from a period fifty or a hundred years from now, but a different sort of time altogether, in which Dr. Hudson and I are not creatures of flesh and blood but mere storybook characters. Such money as you may have has no doubt been issued at some time in the future from this particular present time, and is therefore worthless except possibly to a collector of *curiosa,* hence my comment regarding 'negotiable' money."

Chester was the one who got his wind back first. "Ah—you know, that's not the most probable sort of thing to deduce. Might I ask how you arrived at those conclusions?"

"Though I confess that I myself was somewhat taken aback at my deductions," answered Altamont, smiling briefly, "the means by which I obtained them were simple—straightforward observation logically analyzed."

The coach rounded a curve and swayed sickeningly. The road was getting rougher.

"When you entered," continued Altamont, "and I had my first sight of you, the road dust on your boots showed that you had been wandering through the area for at least a reasonable space of time, and you could not have avoided noting the various artifacts of this era, such as this very coach; you then must have known that you were at a certain general time period in the past, your past, as I presume and certainly hope that our descendants will have designed more effecient means of locomotion than this.

"It was of course obvious, though startling, that you were from the future, since both your clothes and such devices as that miniature recorder which amplifies sound are of a type and quality that our present science and industry are not capable of producing. In the light of this, your reactions to us were quite interesting. It was obvious that you recognized us from your reactions and the expressions you exchanged. Your looks then changed to those of incredulity and disbelief.

"Why would this be? If you were simply from the future I shall know you might possibly have read Dr. Hudson's accounts of my cases. In that event you might reasonably be surprised or even amazed at the coincidence of meeting me here, but you would not disbelieve it or think it impossible, for you would know you were in the past—as I've pointed out—and in this time I obviously exist. Since, however, while recognizing me and Dr. Hudson, you seemed to think it impossible that we actually existed in this time, I was left with but one conclusion and explanation; that we *do* exist in your world, but only as imaginary beings, characters of fiction."

"Amazing!" I said.

"Elementary," said he.

Chester'd lit his own pipe during this explication, and now he leaned forward through a ball of smoke. "Just one thing," he said, "about your names—"

Altamont put a finger to his lips. "Part of my agreement with the Transylvanian government is that I will assist them to avoid publicity by traveling and working under a cognomen, the same to apply to my companion, Dr. 'Hudson.' You now see, I trust, why I asked the good Doctor to help the coachman. He is as stout and true as English oak, but I am very much afraid that if he had heard our little discussion he would have put me down as a hopeless Bedlamite."

"Since you're probably the only person we're likely to meet in this world who won't think *we're* lunatics," I asked, "do you have any suggestions as to how we might get back to our own space and time?"

"It certainly is a pretty little problem," said Altamont abstractedly. Then: "I am not aware of the circumstances of your arrival here, but the situation is so unique I should imagine knowing them would not help a great deal. It would seem that your only logical step would be to duplicate as closely as possible your actions just prior to your leaving your own time."

This could prove difficult. In spite of everything I was still confident enough of our bad luck to be positive that even in this time stream there weren't any vidiphones in turn-of-the-century Transylvania, and *especially* vidiphones gimmicked up by alien invaders. We were pretty quiet for the rest of the journey. Only once did Altamont break the silence. "It occurred to me to ask whether in your world Count Dracula is as fictional as me?"

"He is," affirmed Mike, "but we don't have any story where you encounter him."

Altamont seemed a trifle put out. "What finally happens to him?"

"He's captured and destroyed," answered Mike. "Finished off by a wooden stake through his heart."

"Interesting," said Altamont, "but inapplicable."

It was past eleven when we reached the castle. Not reached it, really; a small stone bridge had collapsed and we had to clamber across a dry river bed and then walk the last hundred yards or so.

The castle was very impressive, as such things go; gothic spires, battlements, arches—if I'd had it back in our own time I could've got rich renting it to Hammer Films as a horror-movie set.

Someone had tried to board up the huge doors, but someone else had ripped them open—with what, I preferred not to think.

The interior, when we cautiously entered, proved to be consistent with the image set forth by the outside appearance; it looked as though it hadn't been lived in for about six centuries. (Slight semantic problem: *How do you refer to a vampire's tenancy? Undeaded in? Immortaled in? Battened down? Vamped?*)

We looked around for some time, tracking through the dust and cobwebs. Coughing, I thought, *if this is how vampires live they'd be right at home in the East Village.* I saw a few things that saw me in turn—a few unhealthily fat rats and, of all things, an armadillo.

It was really quite exceptional in its unlivability. (Why *did* I keep using that sort of word?) The only domicile I'd seen that topped it in this respect was Laszlo Scott's, and then only because Laszlo's place lacked this degree of aesthetic appeal.

"Hey!" Mike trumpeted, and everybody except Altamont jumped a foot. "I found the entrance to the crypt!" Why did he always have to be so damned efficient at this sort of thing?

The entrance was through a huge stone fireplace and down a flight of steps. Luckily there were pitch torches, which flamed up fine at the touch of a match. At the bottom of the steps we paused and tried to peer into the flickering gloom, but the shadows seemed to drink up the light.

Being young and foolish—well, foolish—I was about to venture forward when the silence was broken by a voice from behind us up the stairs. It was high-pitched, oddly accented, and silky.

It said, *"Allow me to introduce myself."*

Somewhere outside, picking up their cue, the wolves began to howl.

12

Well, what do you *think* he looked like?

Right. That's what he looked like.

"I am—Dracula," he said, slowly coming down the steps, and smiling as though he were terribly happy about something. What would he be happy about? I had the distinct feeling that whatever it was it would make me unhappy.

Count Dracula looked at each of us intently, still smiling. "I must apologize for the appearance of my ancestral estate," he said syrupily, "but it has been such a long time since I have entertained visitors—such a *very* long time."

His eyes took on a faraway gaze, as though he were trying to remember that last social occasion long ago and what—or who—had been the main course.

Altamont decided not to let him get too carried away with his memories. "I trust you received notification from your government of my visit here and its purpose."

"But of course," said the Count. "Such rumors! I am greatly disturbed that the wild imaginings of these simple peasant folk should be taken so seriously. Vampires! I have not heard that word used by cultured people for at least two hundred years."

"You don't think, then," asked Altamont, "that there's any evidence that such things exist?"

"Oh, there are stories," laughed the Count, "but nothing you could sink your—but you gentlemen must think me a poor host. Come! I have refreshments awaiting upstairs." With a sweep of his cape the Count turned and led the way back up to the main room.

The table had been cleaned and set by someone or something, and there were five places set. As we took our places Dr. Hudson said, "I say, Altamont, hadn't we better invite the coachman in? He'll be wanting a bit of—"

"Do not concern yourself, Doctor," said the Count. "I have already seen to your driver."

The food smelled quite good but none of our happy little band seemed very hungry. Count Dracula didn't seem to mind; he sat at one end of the table and told us charming little folk tales of beheadings, premature burials, etc. It was as atmospheric as all hell and I didn't like it one little bit.

At the close of the dinner the Count excused himself on some pretext and disappeared through one of the labyrinthine hallways. Dr. Hudson went out to get his medical bag and Altamont gathered us around the dummy fireplace.

"Any thoughts on our host, gentlemen?" he asked.

Michael went first. "Well, he might not be a real vampire, but he's certainly got all the bits of business and set decoration down pat." Mike had always tended to concede by minute degrees, and this sounded suspiciously like the first step.

"And you, Mr. Anderson?"

"I tend to disbelieve on principle any pattern that's this consistent," said Chester. "He's being the Compleat Vampire to the extent of the absurd."

"Mr. Waters?"

"Rrmph. Well, the theological angle has always bothered me, so I don't—hey, wait a minute! Why don't we just wave a crucifix at him and see if he goes *arrgh* and runs away?"

"It would only prove that he's a method actor," Mike pointed out. "Of course we could just drive a stake through his heart, and we'd be able to tell whether he was a vampire or not by what happened to the corpse."

"Michael has," explained Chester to Altamont, "very direct solutions to problems. They're usually more drastic than the problems they solve, but they have the advantage of being tidy."

Altamont looked at the three of us as though he were wondering what he could have been thinking of when he brought us along, and he was just about to say something I was quite sure I didn't want to hear when Dr. Hudson dashed in. "Altamont!" he cried. "Come quickly! You must see the poor devil for yourself!" He ran back out the front entrance, very light on his feet for one of his build, I noted as I puffed out behind everyone else.

The Count was certainly keeping up the old image. The coachman lay beside the carriage, white as a Ku Klux Klan outfit and with two little puncture marks on his neck . . .

Back inside we all had a stiff belt from the Doctor's medicinal flask. I don't drink at all—it makes me sick—but I had decided I would rather feel sick than the only way I'd feel without a bit of a jolt. Altamont mapped out a plan of action. "Dr. Hudson, you will guard the front entrance and the coach. I trust you are prepared?"

The Doctor held up a Western-style revolver. "As you told me, Altamont. Loaded with silver bullets."

I looked at the beautiful workmanship of the gun. "Wherever did you get it?" I asked. Dr. Hudson smiled.

"Odd thing, that," he replied. "I was in a bar, in your San Francisco, when this old Red Indian came up to me and offered both the gun and bullets for an absurdly low price. Said he needed the money to buy whiskey for his paleface friend. Sort of touching, really, and I—"

"Kindly save your reminiscenses for a more convenient time, Dr. Hudson," said Altamont sharply. "Time is of the utmost importance." Without a further word Dr. Hudson left hastily, and Altamont turned to us with a touch of asperity. "These are deep waters, gentlemen," he said sternly, and Chester and Mike looked at me puzzledly for a moment before they caught themselves. "We face a deadly foe, all the more deadly because he himself is of the undead. I should be a fool not to admit it now; the carriage-tracks and spiderwebs told the tale."

"Pardon?" I tried.

"Did you not see?" Altamont gestured impatiently. "There was unblemished moss across the entering carriage path, and vast streamers of webwork filaments. No coach had come near this castle for long before that stone bridge collapsed."

"So?" said Mike. He had been runner-up in the Milford, Pennsylvania, Obtuseness Contest in 1974. If he'd tried a little harder he would have beat me.

"Is it possible you still do not understand?" snapped Altamont. "Surely no human being could travel from the village and negotiate the climb up this mountain, while carrying stores and provisions, on foot. The master of this castle, however, has existed an untold span of time on this barren crag with no sustenance—no sustenance such as we sons of Adam must have to survive. Doubtless our own meal was brought here atop the coach by the driver, already under Count Dracula's influence. Thanks to my bungling," he concluded bitterly, "we shall never hear the truth of that from the coachman's lips."

"You're calling the shots here," said Mike. "What do we do now?"

"Count Dracula must be destroyed, by one means or another," said Altamont. "I am sure he has hidden himself somewhere in the castle to await his opportunity, for he could hardly resist the temptation of five more victims. I shall seek him out in the rooms and towers. In the meanwhile, you three must search the area of the crypt and dungeons, to find the coffin where he sleeps during the hours of light. When you discover it you will render it untenable with this." He handed us each a small bottle of clear liquid. "They were prepared for me in London by Bishop Garrett, a specialist in exorcisms, in the event my tentative hypothesis of mere superstition proved wrong. But we have lost too much time already; we must not waste a moment more."

The three of us started for the fireplace-crypt entrance and Altamont headed for one of the countless staircases. As he reached the foot of the steps he paused and said, "Gentlemen!" We stopped, not used to being called by this particular name, and he added, "should fate and justice fail us and we meet not again, pray accept an Englishman's thanks for assisting him in danger, and a hopeful *bon voyage* to your own time and place." With a brief nod and a smile, Altamont was up the stairs and gone from sight.

Back down in the crypt, we lit as many torches as we could find and started taking a good look around. The only other place

I knew of that was this large and still had such a strong odor of musty decay was the Washington Square subway station, but the subway station didn't have all these coffins—yet, anyway.

"There are so *many* of them!" Mike wailed. "How're we going to find the right one?"

"I hate to say it," said Chester, "but we'll just have to look around until we find an empty."

"What do we do then?" I growled, "take it back to the local funeral parlor and ask them to return the deposit? How will we know it's the right one? I'd think vampires would always have a few spares somewhere around."

Chester looked at me and smiled horribly. "Do you have any better ideas, T. Waters?"

I started checking the coffins.

Ten minutes later, we gave up. Apparently the housing situation was no better for vampires in Transylvania than it was for hippies in New York. Mike, through some sixth sense I'd rather not think about, had discovered the entrance to the dungeons in the meantime, so we gathered up our torches and went down *another* flight of steps.

Right at the bottom was what seemed to be the play-and-torture area, circular in shape, with the cells making a three-quarter ring around its edge. In the central part were a rack, an iron maiden, a wheel, and other such toys, and it was all too obvious that they had been used a great deal at one time or another.

I looked at it in nervous awe. "Andy Blake will never forgive us for not bringing him along, when we tell him about this."

"*If* we tell him about this," Chester corrected. Pessimist.

Tearing ourselves away from the exhibit, we started checking the cells for the Count's wooden sleeping bag. For some reason, which I will refrain from pointing out, the three of us went together into each cell to search it. Tactically, this was not the best idea, but we weren't thinking about tactics until a cell door suddenly slammed behind us.

We all spun around at once. Standing just as we had first seen him, except for the rather Prussian touch of a monocle, was Count Dracula.

"I see that you have managed to find your guest room without my assistance," he said smilingly. He liked to smile; he was very proud of his teeth. "I trust you will be comfortable until I can attend to each of you personally. First, however, I must see to your friend, Mr. Altamont. I believe he is searching for me and I would not wish to disappoint him."

The Count was just turning to go when I pulled out the bottle of liquid Altamont had given me, but with a movement so fast I didn't even see it Dracula reached through the bars and snatched it from my hand. When he saw what it was he laughed and uncorked it. "How thoughtful of Mr. Altamont," he cried, "and yet how insulting!"

He drank half the bottle at one pull. With a judicious air, he said, "It is an interesting little exorcism—rather pretentious, of course, and lacking the richness and power of our native Transylvanian elixirs, but I suppose satisfactory for unimportant occasions." With a sneer of contempt he dashed the bottle to the stone floor and swept away up the stairs, his evening cape trailing behind him.

It was fully five minutes before any of us could speak, and naturally I was the one that finally did. "We certainly seem to have done it this time."

"Sure you're not overstating the case?" gibed Mike.

"That I do by profession," I answered, "but in this case, no."

Chester looked around. "This place is somewhat old," he said in his best proto-hipster tradition. "It can't *possibly* be as solid as it once was."

We were in the process of proving that theory wrong, Chester checking the window bars and Mike and I at the front of the cell, when Chester said softly, "Oh, Good Lord." We joined him at the window and after a look at what he was seeing began to wonder about that theological judgment.

Not twenty yards from us and in full view, Count Dracula and the man we called Altamont faced each other at the edge of a precipice that fell away in a sheer wall to the valley below. Altamont was holding a long wooden stick with a sharpened point, and seemed to be shielding his eyes. The Count was approaching him step by step, but Altamont made no move to raise the stick toward his adversary.

Slowly, agonizingly, Altamont raised his head to stare Dracula full in the face, and even from our distance we could see the blank, mindless expression in the detective's eyes.

Smiling cruelly, Count Dracula stepped forward and reached for the now-wavering stick. Then it happened.

With a trained swordsman's lightning thrust, Altamont plunged the pointed stick deep into Count Dracula's breast. The vampire screeched, an unbelievable wailing, rending sound. He tottered forward, the huge wound gushing stolen blood, and locked Altamont in his grasp. Altamont locked his own arms about the inhuman thing, and without hesitation stepped backward off the ledge.

The last moment we could see him, before he and the vampire of Castle Dracula vanished from sight, Altamont's face was alight with triumph.

13

I t was several minutes later when we noticed that we had all been crying, and when we did none of us were the least bit ashamed of it.

Strangely, or maybe not so strangely, it was a couple of hours before we started thinking about our own situation again. For a while we shouted at the top of our lungs, in the hope that Dr. Hudson would hear us; but as the time went by with no results we began to realize that Altamont had not destroyed Dracula before the Count had claimed another victim.

Continuing our check of the walls and bars took us until past dawn, and when we finally sat down on the stone floor we knew that the cell was solid enough to hold us—or our remains—for a long, long time.

No; not exactly.

For a long, long *this* time.

"Hey, listen," I said, as though Chester and Mike had any choice, "I've just had a thought."

"Odder things will happen in moments of stress," observed Chester. "Say on."

"I'm not quite sure myself just what this means, but we're only trapped here because of the time situation; this whole thing is just fiction in our own world, so if we could only . . ." I trailed off.

"With solutions such as yours, T. Waters, we don't need problems." Chester turned to Mike. "Hit him for me, will you?"

Michael shook his head. "I'm too tired." He looked at his hand as though he expected it to turn on him. "Besides, that's not what bothers me. Tom has just inadvertently reminded me of something that was just coming to the surface when we saw that—the scene at the window."

"?" Chester and I grunted in unison.

"The language," said Michael. "It should be Serbo-Croat, or a Russian dialect, or *something* like that—we're in Transylvania, aren't we?—but it isn't. It's English; we heard the bartender and a couple of other people." I started to object but Mike forestalled me. "It isn't coincidence. Remember that stagecoach? It said 'TRANSYLVANIAN OVERLAND LINES'—English words in English script instead of foreign words in Cyrillic."

"And what do you conclude from that?" inquired Chester, who had somehow managed to keep his pipe through all this and was carefully filling it.

"Nothing yet," Mike muttered, "but it's got to mean something."

"I'll tell you what bothers me," I said. "That armadillo."

"What could an armadillo possibly do to bother you?" asked Michael.

"A number of things, I imagine," I said, "but this one did it just by being here. Armadillos aren't native to this part of the world at all. They can't survive in this climate."

"That one seemed to be doing pretty well," Chester said between puffs. "Besides, I'm not sure you're right about that. If I remember correctly, in the Lugosi film of *Dracula* that Tod Browning did way back in the Thirties, the one they show on the idiot lantern every so often, among the other creepy crawlies was a genuine armor-plated armadillo."

"THAT'S *IT*!" I cried, and Chester and Mike both jumped a foot. "This whole thing, that's what's wrong with it. *It isn't real at all, in any time.* It's like a story or a movie, and the people speak English and act the way we expect them to for the same reason as the impossible armadillo being around—because the whole thing is from our own heads!"

After a pause Chester said, "That shouldn't be too difficult to test. Let's all concentrate on that cell door opening—no, better yet, don't look at it. It isn't there. Never was there. This cell just never had a door, that's all."

After a few seconds of glassy-eyed silence there was a

PDING!

and we looked.

No cell door. Never had been. There were little cobwebs in the corners of the cell doorway where there had never been a door.

"My, my," said Chester as we walked out into the central room. "My, my."

Michael was exploring the possibilities of this. "Why don't we imagine that there was always going to be a nice big meal waiting for us when we went upstairs?"

"Certainly worth a try," I agreed, "but we'll have to agree on the menu."

Chester intervened. He would. "This is all very well and good, children, but I think it might be more constructive (you will forgive the pun, I know) if we were to imagine that somewhere in this room, with its own power source, is a vidip like the one in Mystic Jake's apartment."

We had to concede that it was a somewhat more direct solution than food. We sat down and started believing.

"It isn't going to work, Chester," I intoned after ten minutes with no results. "The damn things are just too complicated."

"Maybe we're doing it the hard way," said Mike. "Let's try this: I'll concentrate on the wiring, you, Thomas, work on its outside appearance, and Chester works on the sounds it made."

Ignoring the implied slight of Mike's classification, I set to work concentrating.

Nothing happened for a few seconds, and then a hazy shape started to appear in outline on the stone floor, sort of like an erector set made out of smoke. It had the vague look of the vidip, but just as it seemed to be getting ready to become more palpable it suddenly disappeared completely.

This happened about four times.

"I know what our problem is," I said, knowing what our problem was. "We're watching, and every time the damn thing starts to appear it breaks our concentration. Eyes closed this time."

It took longer than the cell door, of course, but less then half a minute had passed when

BLARSHHHHHHHHHHHH

and there stood a vidip just like the one in Mystic Jake's.

Really just like. Our subconscious minds must've noted every detail, for this vidip was complete with a light coating of grime and a pair of meandering cockroaches.

Chester was pleased. "Now, Michael, if you will do whatever it was you did before, maybe we will return to our proper place."

I certainly hoped not; I just wanted to get back to where we came from.

It took Mike a few seconds to find the proper wires, and then there was another short delay when we realized that we had forgotten to provide the power source. Chester abstained while Mike and I fervently believed in an old army surplus field generator. Naturally, it took two or three tries before we got one that was in working condition, but finally we were all set. Chester and I each held an end of wire while Mike probed about. "It happened when I pulled off one of the wires," he explained. "I'm not sure, but I think it may have been

ZZAP!

this one."

We looked around dazedly. The dungeon and everything else had disappeared in a silvery flash, and there was a feeling like the one you get when an Up elevator slows.

We were standing on a sand dune and it was hot. Oh, hot. Hot like I had no idea was permitted outside certain theological concepts. There was a sand dune in front of us and a sand dune behind us. There was another sand dune on the left and still another on the right. All around these sand dunes were a lot more sand dunes. We were, I decided, in a desert.

Not your ordinary garden-variety desert, either. This one was fully equipped with tanks.

There were a lot more of them than we could have counted, had we cared to, and they seemed rather evenly divided into two groups, one labeled with a swastika and the other with a Union Jack. They were blasting away at each other with great verve and style.

Chester and I looked at Mike accusingly. "Neither Chester nor I know enough about tanks to dream up anything like this," I said, "so either we'd better get out of here or you had better be able to imagine a better tank than either of those."

Mike protested his innocence loudly and unconvincingly, and it was so entertaining that we might've listened to it all day if there hadn't been a war beside us. As it was, the racket from the tank cannons made it nearly impossible to concentrate, and if everybody hadn't stopped to reload at the same time we might never have left. As soon as we'd produced the vidip we hurriedly grabbed the wires and

ZZAP!

again; this time it seemed a little later than before, but that was only because the forest was shading us from the sunlight.

"*Who R U?*" enquired the Caterpillar haughtily, staring down from his perch on a rather magnificent mushroom. It blew a cloud of psychedelically decorated smoke in our direction, which Chester sniffed with the judicial air of an Escoffier.

"A little Acapulco Gold there," he decided, "but I wish I knew where he scores."

"From the Cheshire Cat?" offered Mike.

I rejected this. "With a smile like his the Cheshire Cat has got to be a speed freak."

"*WHO R U?*" The Caterpillar was getting annoyed.

Chester, as The Man Who Knew The Butterfly Kid, seemed the logical choice to be our Caterpillar spokesman. "Just tourists, Sir," he replied, eyeing the Caterpillar's water pipe a bit wistfully.

The answer didn't seem to impress the Caterpillar at all. He sat there puffing away and stared at us; not many people can claim to have been stared down by a caterpillar.

We backed away uncertainly into the forest.

"I suggest, gentlemen," said Chester, "that we try to keep our minds on our proper destination this time. If another miss puts us in one of *my* more vivid memories we'll be lucky to ever get back."

The vidip appeared almost instantly this time; practice was perfect making.

ZZAP!

We took a long look round at the depressing and morbid vista about us, and breathed a sigh of relief.

We were back in Mystic Jake's pad.

"There's something I'd better check," said Mike, and gingerly avoiding the dangling wires, he got up from his original position and moved to the front of the console. He punched a service combo and an amorphous voice informed us that it was a little before nine in the evening; same date, and only a few seconds later than when we had—left? I didn't know for sure now, and I was even more uncertain when we found that our watches tallied with the time service. This discovery had affected Mike in a somewhat different way. He was looking at the machine with an expression I was quite sure I wasn't going to like when I knew the reason for it.

"Now if this whole thing didn't really happen," he said, talking to the vidip in his Now-Here's-My-Plan voice as though it were the one he had to convince, "then it could be the biggest thing in show business since—ah—talkies." Mike's rhetoric can be inspired. "We could have, like, booths for people, and—"

"What would you call it?" I said, interrupting his semicolloquy. "Lifeys and Deathies?"

Chester agreed with me; he must've been a bit more shaken than I'd thought. "The problem here, M. T. Bear, is that we have no idea of what would have happened if we hadn't figured out a little of what was happening, enough to get back, anyway. We might have, in terms of here and now, simply disappeared, or we might be insane, or bodies with no minds. A bit unpredictable, wouldn't you agree?"

I couldn't have said it better myself, so I didn't. "There's also," I pointed out, "a somewhat more pressing matter: our dear friend Mystic Jake and his silly putty pals."

With a little sigh Mike stepped back from the vidip. "Show biz," he said wistfully, "it'll just have to wait. Well, I'll tell you one thing; I'm not going to try to disarm this thing again. We were lucky to get back before, I guess, and who knows what could happen if I pull another wrong wire?"

"A point. By all means do not pull another wire." Not, you understand, that I had any fear for my own life. No, it was possible that the Alien's vidip could alter time for everyone, or maybe explode, or do who knew what unpredictable things to humanity.

Also the damned thing was making me very nervous; if I was nice to it maybe it wouldn't hurt me.

Mike looked askance. He could look more askance than anyone else I knew. "In that case what *do* we do?"

In a harmony worthy of John Cage, Chester and I replied, "We go make plans."

What else?

It was going to be one of *those* evenings again, as if it hadn't already been enough of one. After debating options a bit we'd decided to head back toward the Midway, as Bleecker-MacDougal was called, so we'd be more in touch with our sources of random-access information if anything might happen.

An interesting aspect of whatever the vidip had done to us was that we weren't at all tired; even Mike, who'd been sleepy to begin with, was wide awake and ready for the evening's adventures.

By some fluke of conversation we had actually formulated a vague strategy by the time we reached the Main Drag (on nights when it was this crowded that phrase had two descriptive senses), and this plan was roughly along the lines of Divide and Loiter. Mike would station himself in the Nobody, Chester in the What's That?, and I, somewhat reluctantly, would return to the Pentalpha, where I'd no doubt have to do another set.

'Twas a far, far better thing I was doing than I had ever intended to do.

Weinie was in his accustomed warren behind the cash register, and when I made an entrance mistimed between Piltdown's sets he threw a line in a stage whisper that sounded like a King Cobra with laryngitis. "Honored Master of Destiny! Grace our stage with your presence and divine the problems of these anxious people!" I did a Hollywood-Thirties-movie salaam to our—dammit!—packed house and headed for the back room. As I passed by him Weinie muttered, "Yabumyanevarounatatrowyout," making it sound like a single word in a language no one would want to learn.

My crystal ball was on the floor under the sink, and the two waterbugs were trying to shove it through a hole far too small for it while the cockroach supervised. It was a very creditable effort and I hated to discourage it but that was my only crystal; I scooped it up and apologized to the trio.

They took it rather hard, and sat there under the sink glaring at me while I finished getting ready for my set; then they stomped off for what looked like a council of war, and I hoped vaguely that they weren't any better at it than we had been.

Weinie gave me the low sign and I went out to get the thing over with, thinking idly that if I got much more tired of doing this it would be almost as bad as work. It might have the saving grace of being moderately fraudulent, but work all the same. Harrowing; I was using up my avenues of sloth at an alarming rate.

Down through the dim corridors of time . . .

Checking over the tide-pool like sea of faces I noted a few familiar ones here and there, and a pair of others that could've been pretty familiar if they'd wanted to. Wendy was there, and Big Tex; Alphonse, the ancient and bearded newsie who'd been hawking papers and magazines in the coffeehouses for longer than anyone dared remember; Amy, but no Frederick; assorted random guitars with the standard folknik attachment; and Velia, a prime example of sweet young thing, red-haired variety, who suffered from an identity crisis—Velia couldn't decide whether she was a sprite or a witch.

Q: I have lots of little troubles . . .

A: Have you tried insecticides?

Arghhh. It really *was* getting to me.

I waded through the set with my mind submerged, and wrapped it up as quickly as I decently could. The tourist segment of the audience applauded uncertainly and, having sipped once or twice at the incomprehensible coffee, paid their incomprehensible checks and departed. Uncomprehendingly.

Wendy and Tex waved me to their table, and I sank down into the chair until my eyes were about level with the tabletop. The view was uninspiring but it fitted in beautifully with my state of mind.

Tex, so nicknamed because he comes from Brooklyn, is large enough to conceal small girls about his person and has been known to do that from time to time. I looked at what he was assembling on the table. "Where'd you pick up the Schmeisser?"

He inserted the clip and checked the action of the bolt. "Well, you know how it is, people always dropping by with old war souvenirs." He looked up at me. "Besides, I'm getting ready for the invasion."

Hot (insert favored expletive)!

"What invasion is that?" Innocently, as befits my character.

Tex stuck the Schmeisser into a canvas bag. "The way I heard, you know all about it; some sort of flying-saucer thing, people coming down and making themselves look like us." He laughed. "Some people'll do *anything* to win a war."

Absolutely enchanting. So now probably everyone in the Village had the explanation of the replicating, and whatever happened next would be without benefit of Chester, Mike, or I laying even a fake groundwork to avoid panic.

Avoid panic; I really thought that, and my mind snurgled around with ways to alter the situation. Well, a rumor was a rumor, and a false one could replace a true one just as easily as if the vice were versa. "Oh, that," I laughed, "don't you know the real story on that?"

Tex shook his head and Wendy looked up from her crocheting. *Crocheting?* "Now I'd like to find out what's been going on too."

"Ah, well, now, that duplicating," I said, blathering on and being surprised that the words kept coming out, "that's all another thing—ah—doesn't have anything to do with the saucers and invaders. Mike and I made up the invasion thing—we're working on a gag to do at the party."

"*Party?*" Wendy dropped four purls, or knits, or whatever it is you drop.

"—ah, you remember, don't you, the party? No? Oh, well, it's tonight around midnight over at Mike's. You're both invited, of course."

Wendy jumped in the air with the sort of squeal she usually made under less public circumstances and dashed out, dragging Tex behind her. I knew full well that it would be a matter of much less than an hour before everyone any of us knew, even at first or second remove, had been informed of the festivities, and this would hopefully cancel out the invasion talk, or at least take it out of active consideration until Chester, Mike, and I could get together and—what was it we had to do to save the world—ah, yes, Make A Plan.

After a brief colloquy with Amy that involved her trying to crawl into my ear tongue first, and my wondering just *exactly* how well she knew Wendy, and my standard one-minute haggle with Weinie over the head count during my set, I shifted into Low Trundle and headed for The Nobody, where Mike would presumably still be controlling his strategic demesne. We had things to do before our guests arrived.

I was speculating idly on what Mike's reaction to this would be—he hated parties only slightly less than Chester and I—when a sort of subliminal alarm went off in my head, the kind that warns you when you're about to step into a pile of dog extranea, and I ground to a halt.

"Wha's happenin', baby?" asked Mystic Jake.

14

This was an eventuality for which I hadn't properly prepared myself.

Not that that was particularly surprising; I'd long ago figured out that the things that happened to me were, generally speaking, the kind you *couldn't* prepare for. Encountering Mystic Jake was a prime example of this sort of thing; what preparation could one make for meeting Jake, except catatonia or suicide?

The lights of MacDougal were reflected from Jake's shiny surfaces—his hair, eyes, nose, and the knees of his trousers. I was, unfortunately, downwind of him, and the strong pine-and-alcohol scent of cheap shaving lotion didn't quite disguise the less mentionable smells it was riding on. Perhaps a fir tree might have liked it, but all it did for me was force me to change my position relative to the wind.

"Yeah, man, what's happening?" I riposted neatly. (This particular catchphrase-type question has lately fallen into disuse, at least among those who know Chester, Mike, and me; whenever some unsuspecting soul asks it we answer him, and one of Chester's answers took seven hours and twenty-two minutes—he later sold it, carefully edited, to Grove Press.)

"Uh—hey man, you still lookin' for the little green men from Mars?" Jake was being Subtle, which was only laughable; when he was straightforward he was incomprehensible.

I decided that it wouldn't be of much use, no matter how enjoyable, to let Jake know the way of things. "Little green men? Oh, yes, I remember that business. It was just a pill that was going around that gave people schizoid hallucinations, and a lot of people picked up on it in a contact high sort of way."

This, of course, made no sense at all, especially in view of Jake's little fairy tale at the Nobody a couple of nights before, but I knew Jake well enough to predict his reaction to this. He'd try to figure it out, five seconds being his attention span, and then he'd just give up on it and say *oh*.

About seven seconds went by and then Jake said, "Oh."

See?

"Yeah, well, that's cool then, man. It's all cool, then, yeah, man?" When Jake's brain had found enough words to make a sentence, it hated to let them go and start all over again.

"Far as I know, Jake, everything's back to normal. Just one of those things." But Jake wasn't going to give up quite yet.

"What's this I hear about Kurland havin' a bear?" I didn't think Jake had figured out any connection with his plotting; he probably wanted to tell Mike that he could get him on the Ed Sullivan show. Still, I didn't want to give anything away just yet, even inadvertently.

I gave Jake an Understanding-Comrade-in-Arms smile, which broke something inside of me, and said, "Jake." One-beat pause. "You *know* Mike."

It was only three seconds to the *oh* this time, so perhaps Jake *was* giving up, or, more improbably, beginning to realize that he wasn't getting anywhere.

With a smiling wave of dismissal that indicated my audience was at an end, he turned and moved off uncertainly into the crowd, trailing a piney miasma.

Difficult, very difficult it was to believe that anyone or anything intent on conquering the world would decide on Mystic Jake as their pet Benedict Arnold. Naturally—because it was hard to think of *any* use or function for Jake that something else couldn't do better. Even as a target for gibes and one-liners from the rest of us Jake was less than satisfactory, since there was no challenge; insulting him was shooting a fish in a barrel.

I trundled toward the What's That? to pick up Chester before going on to the Nobody, since Mike's body was very Newtonian: when at rest it tended to remain at rest.

Why *had* the Aliens picked Mystic Jake? Either it was a complete random choice of incredible bad luck (for them), which seemed unlikely, or it was because of some quality or characteristic that Jake possessed, which seemed even less likely.

It wouldn't be too difficult, I thought, for invaders from another planet or another country to suborn or corrupt or coerce someone into being a traitor, given a few chances to find the proper type for their purposes. Back in my spy days (ah, youth!) I'd taught a class in the techniques, and I admitted to myself now that traitors generally didn't have to be very clever or even helpful, but usually just a front or a go-between—always very carefully controlled.

How were the Aliens controlling Jake? I speculated: Blackmail? Impossible. Things people would blackmail Mystic Jake with were the things he bragged about. Money? Oddly, I didn't think so. Jake would do almost anything for bread within his own hustler's framework, but even he would realize that a successful invasion would change things into a rigidly-ordered society where (a) his money wouldn't mean much, if anything, and (b) he wouldn't be able to hustle.

Power? It seemed to be the only thing left, and it might find a home in what we will, for laughs, call Jake's consciousness, but it still didn't sound right. Maybe he didn't really know what the Aliens were up to, or realize they were serious—or maybe— the final possibility floated into view, glittering with irony— maybe he was willing to sell the world in order to be needed, just once.

In that case his situation was sad and I had sympathy—but the price of the imminent act of psychotherapy was just a bit steep.

Chester was in the far corner of the What's That? where he was somewhat protected from the decibly-exhibited enthusiasm of The Kwikantha Dead, the house rock group. Some familiar faces, and other faces that tried to look familiar but only succeeded in looking misplaced, were grouped around the battered oak table, all in a state of reverent awe for one of Chester's impromptu dissertations. He was, to counterfeit a phrase, the cynosure of all eyes.

"Evening, cynosure," I screamed above the even-here hellish din, and bullied a chair from one of the Sub-Elect. He nodded as I sat down, and continued speaking. I was right next to him and could just barely make some of it out; the people on the other side of the table must have been either lip readers or telepaths.

". . . forms of music that were once . . . synthesis . . . creating a pattern . . . causality . . . inner consciousness forming its own sensory experience . . . control of . . . acausal . . . synchronicity . . . tone analysis . . . disruption . . . *I Ching* . . . furthers one . . . in the fourth place . . . no blame." He sat back with a contented expression and sipped something that looked like a pregnancy test on the rocks.

At that moment, naturally, the music stopped, either because the K-Dead had got tired of playing or because the din had set up a harmonic field and they'd all disintegrated. I had my dreams.

"How's that again?" I inquired.

"How was it before?" Chester countered.

"Your little class here," I persisted, gesturing around the now-depopulating table. "What was all that in aid of?"

Chester gave me a look of patient and benign pity. It was one of his standards, and I had a whole trunkful at home, but he seemed to think I needed it. "T. Waters," he doctrinaired, "by now you really should have perceived the underlying patterns in this sort of thing, as it applies to minor celebrities such as myself and even more minor—less major?—figures such as yourself." He peered through the pregnancy test to confirm that we were nominally alone. "There is conversation and there is dissertation. Conversation is what our happy little band has amongst its members; dissertation is the way we generally talk when there's anyone else around, and it's usually for their benefit and pseudo-edification. The little bit I was doing with somewhat more blatant staging than usual just now was about how music will take over the world."

"?"

"Who remembers?" said Chester. "Of course, if you'd like me to make up a theory . . .

"I suspect I'll be able to survive without it, at least for now," I said hurriedly. "Listen, there's sort of a new development . . ."

"A *party*?" Chester yelped as we fought the current and made slow progress along Bleecker, after I had told him what had happened with Tex and Wendy. "I mean: saving the world is all very well, it's one of the few occupations where I've got job experience, and I'm perfectly willing to help, but . . . a *party*?"

"Now, now, Chester, it won't be all that bad," I lied blandly. "Wait'll we pick up Mike and I will explain the whole raisin daughter of the thing."

"Ha!" retorted Chester. "It's supposed to be at his place, hey? I can just imagine what his reaction will be to that."

Mmm. I could imagine it myself, two or three times before breakfast, without straining at all. Mike, like Chester and I, had an aversion to parties, but he made a fetish of it. "Nothing to do with parties as such," he would carefully explain. "Why, as a matter of fact I sort of like them. That party in *The Thin Man*, the William Powell-Myrna Loy movie, is one of my favorites." This established, Mike would continue: "It's the *people*—there just aren't enough people around to make a good party where you don't have some bums and drags and everybody getting uptight."

(Parenthetical Sociological Note: Our real reason was, I suspected, common to the three of us, and related to what Chester had been saying a short while before. We were simply compulsive performers, and while this wasn't so bad in the coffee houses where people were constantly drifting in and out, at Village parties that usually lasted two or three days it would be a bit of a strain. Better to avoid the temptation in the first place.)

(Second Parenthetical Note: Why, you may well ask, do I stop to explain the above rather minor point? Ah, yes, well may you ask. For one thing, to begin, it reveals the motivation behind a subsequent off-stage conversation, and I felt that at this point in my report of our activities a little motivation was needed, however abstract. For another reason, it may provide the reader with an explanation of certain cloudy conversations in his own experience as well as some of those found here. In addition to being therefore educational it gives the report a redeeming social value, which may come in handy if I should decide to put in some pornography later on. Besides, if you've read this far you've committed yourself by blowing your time, and every third reader your money, so quit grumbling and read on . . .)

As it happened, Chester and I were both wrong about Mike's reaction, thwarted in our calculations by Situational

Default. It happened that when we arrived Mike was in Earnest Conversation with a pair of outlander females and, having jacked out of them necessary operational data (phone, availability, etc.), was proceeding along approved Von Clausewitzian lines by consolidating his position. We inadvertently deprived him of the charm of novelty when we were introduced ("Oh, *you're* writers *too*? Isn't that *wonderful*?), but Mike didn't seem to notice much. Our hushed entreaties and whispers fit in nicely with the image he had selected for their benefit, so he came quietly. It wasn't until we were almost at his pad that the horrible reality of the situation sank in.

"A party? They'll actually be inside the apartment, all of them?" Mike was trying hard not to understand.

"That's the way it's usually done," I admitted. "Look, it won't be so bad, and besides, with Tex and Wendy spreading the word, by now it's too far gone to stop anyway."

Mike opened the door with his homemade Magna-Key circuit and we went in. "Now that's not necessarily true," he said with a macabre edge to his voice. "We could—oh, all right, I'll throw the damn thing, but you could at least give me something that I could use as an excuse to myself."

I explained what had happened back at the Pentalpha, and added, "in addition to providing some protective coloring for that whole series of incidents, it just might generate some sort of crisis."

Mike stopped. *"Crisis,* you say?" he echoed, and looked at me uncertainly. "The last time you had us start using that as an operational procedure we were nearly torn apart by that berserk circus crowd."*

"No, no, I didn't mean anything that drastic," I soothed. "It's simply that with a goodly number of the local people who've encountered the Aliens in one shape or another, said invaders might very well make some sort of move."

"You don't consider that drastic?" asked Chester.

"No," I answered. "Since even in the unlikely event that the Aliens *do* show up they're not likely to do anything violent. After

---

* See *The Unicorn Girl*

all, if they were that way inclined, and have the technology we think they do, they could wipe us all out. And, of course, there's that conversation I overheard, from the Alien who was posing as me—all that stuff about staying with the Pattern, *et* and *cetera*—it seemed to indicate that they have a very particular way of going about things, so past experience of them indicates that now, at least, we won't be in any real danger."

"There's also the point," Mike commented, "that their sticking to the Pattern can help us a lot, because (a) if we find out what the Pattern is, even if they know we know, they'll have to stick to it, and (b) if this pattern is a straight-line sort of thing, all we have to do is stop it once—we don't have to worry about other things they might do."

"True," confirmed Chester reluctantly. "I must admit that their Pattern seems godawful important to them. They certainly seemed down on one of their own in that bit you overheard— what did they call him,—Solidus Plim?—so perhaps they've given us an edge. Whether it's enough of one is another question."

I had stopped listening, and by the time Chester was finished speaking I had folded in the customary places and was sitting on the floor holding my head. I was ambivalent about this; if I didn't hold it, my head might very well drop off and roll along the floor, but why keep something attached to my body that hurt this much?

"You have a headache," Mike pronounced, and headed for the Pharmachest.

"Aaaaaahhhhhhhh, yooooo ahoowah sooooooornly dooooo," I confirmed succinctly. Mike came back with a capsule and a glass of water, and in a few seconds fast, fast, Fast pain relief was speeding toward my headache. Of course, it took the usual ten minutes or so to get there, but it *did* start off impressively.

"What happened to you?" Mike asked finally, when I was more or less in working order again.

"I had a headache." Brilliant.

"You don't generally get them like that," Mike persisted, "so what set this one off?"

Thinking very gingerly, so's not to hurt my brain, I considered this. "Well, Chester was talking—talking—and he had just mentioned Solidus Plim . . ." As soon as I said the name there was a dull throb in my forehead that pulsed for a few seconds and then stopped.

"Solidus Plim," I said. ". . . yes, he, or whatever he is, he's the problem that set me off. There's something I feel I ought to remember about him, something that bothers me."

"Something you *ought* to remember?" asked Chester. "Why should you know anything about an Alien?"

"That's what bothers me." I stood up, did a ten-count while my head joined me, and took a look around. "We're going to have to hop to it if there's really going to be a party around here." The refrigerator and cupboard were in Mike's usual Mother Hubbard state; Chester trotted out to an all-night deli in the area after we'd made a grocery list governed by the classification Lot Of, But Cheap.

Mike and I, meanwhile, arranged what little there was to arrange, picked out strategic points for ourselves, and slid an ancient secretary-cabinet in front of Mike's bedroom door to remove it and its contents from random access. (This wasn't really overprotective paranoia; at Village parties only about a fourth of the people that show up are people you know, and they're usually not the fourth you invited.)

Finally we surveyed our handiwork, and then plopped down to wonder what wonders would wander into our wondrous world.

We weren't going to be disappointed.

15

We hadn't really expected such a mob to show up, but parties that year had been sort of scarce, and parties thrown by *us* were a unique phenomenon; most of our guests, I suspected, were here more out of morbid curiosity.

The party had idled for about three-quarters of an hour, and then Wendy appeared with a huge box of freshly-baked and much-fabled brownies. Not long after, the action had shifted into High, and I found myself being very impressed with my own brilliance, the heavy erotical quotient of the chicks, the great decor of Mike's pad . . .

Decor of Mike's pad? Oh wow, those brownies of Wendy's were even stronger than I'd suspected.

Chester had inveigled one of his pet barock groups into dropping by, and after adjusting their arrangements to the resistance capacity of Mike's fusebox they began to play, and very sedately, I observed.

But then, I couldn't hear too well because Wendy was trying to get into my ear again.

Everything drifted along nicely, the walls swaying in gentle response to the music, most everyone in varying stages of enchantment and undress, a soft aromatic haze undulating a few feet from the ceiling . . .

A few hours passed and the gathering hit a temporary lull, the first shift of people having for the most part departed and the Second Strike force not at our target area yet. Chester was rapping with the barock group, and Mike and I were having a discussion so vague we couldn't even remember what it was about *during* it, while our respective ladies fair compared notes on the past few hours with occasional whoops and mysterious giggles. Hrmph.

There was a floor lamp of what appeared to be about mid-Thirties vintage standing against the wall behind us, and apparently it couldn't take it any longer. It sidled forward, if a lamp can be said to sidle, and beckoned us to follow it outside. No one else in the room seemed to notice anything strange about this if they saw it at all—most of them had never been to Mike's pad.

We dutifully toddled out behind the lamp; it moved back in the corner behind the stairwell where we wouldn't be seen. Aha, thought I, this lamp has not been in the Village scene for very long—retiring types and shrinking violets had a high ego-mortality rate.

The lamp spoke, although we couldn't quite see how it was doing it. "I'm afraid I don't quite know how to break this to you," it began hesitantly, twining its pull-chains nervously, "but your race is about to be invaded by beings from another world— another star system, in fact. You see—"

"Is *that* all?" I scoffed. "We've known that for a long time. Old stuff." For some reason I was feeling very good, and having our nice party interrupted by a lamp to tell me something I already knew was merely an annoyance.

Damn those brownies.

Mike confirmed my scoff with a pitying shake of his head, and we patted the lamp reassuringly on the shade and returned to the front room.

Luckily, as I realized a while later and straighter, the as-'twere lamp was not about to be put off. We had just made ourselves comfy again in the living room when a vacuum cleaner at full blast came rolling into the room. I sensed vaguely that something wasn't quite right, because Mike hadn't had a vacuum cleaner since the time some months back when he'd tried to convert his into a bazooka that would shoot around corners, and in grand fashion had not quite succeeded.

The vacuum cleaner moved purposefully over to a position just behind Chester, who couldn't have avoided hearing it unless he was playing something like *I Ching, You Chang, They Chung* on the group's electric harpsichord—which, of course, he was.

The vacuum cleaner struck like a cobra—a very fat cobra—its tube going under Chester's arm and to the top of the harpsichord, where his recorder pot pipe was resting. In an instant the instrument had been snarfled into the bowels of the vacuum, and it retreated coyly out of sight into the hallway as Chester, in a shocked trance, followed.

A goodly time, although we were in no position to judge, went by before Chester reappeared, holding his beloved pipe and looking what is, for him, even more studious and thoughtful than usual.

"The vacuum cleaner," he said nodding in the direction of the hall, "says we're about to be—"

"Oh, c'mon, now, Chester," Mike interrupted. "We've heard all that from the lamp. Old stuff. It couldn't take over the world anyway; why, even in Europe it couldn't run off house current without an adapter." This, although at least paralogical, sounded strange even to me, and I thought about the brownies. Hmm.

"*Scusami,*" I interjected, and went to the vidip and punched out a number I knew well. The screen glowed lambently for a couple of buzzes, and then it was illuminated with a familiar face.

"Hi, love," said Wendy. "What's happening?"

Zappo. Instant down.

"It might take a long time to explain that . . . ah, what've you been doing?"

Wendy looked at me rather strangely. "Well, I *was* going to come to the party, but then Mike called to say it was off, so I've just been sitting all alone by the vidiphone, pushing my gitbox through Volume Four of *English and Scottish Popular Ballads.*"

After a while she said, "Anything wrong?"

"Hmm? Ah, no, not really—there was just a little confusion about something. Listen, I'll give you a buzz later." "But—"

"B'bye, love. Hold your guitar and think of me." As the screen faded to black I stood there and wondered; and what have *I* been doing more than holding for the past couple of hours? My, as

Chester would say, my. There are people who don't approve of what they call miscegenation—what indeed would they think of what had just happened to me? I thought about the more vivid parts of my little *tête-à-tête* with, er, Null-Wendy, and my respect for the abilities of the Aliens increased considerably.

It wasn't too difficult to speculate on what had happened; it had probably begun with Mystic Jake finding out about the party and, suspecting something, warning his superiors—pardon me, bosses. *Superiors,* applied in relation to Jake, was far too broad a term.

Mike and Chester were still talking about the vacuum cleaner when I went back into the front room, but a quick look around revealed that Null-Wendy was long-gone, and this didn't surprise me a great deal. Well, it would be prudent to apprise Mike and Chester of this new subplot and its implications.

I didn't immediately get the opportunity.

No sooner had I plopped down on what Mike kept insisting was a mattress than there was a slight bit of commotion in the hall and the latest entry in our Dadaist Sweepstakes came rolling in. It was a small color 3V set on one of those castered metal stands they have so you can push them around the room. This particular one was doing fine without any outside help. It rolled to a stop in front of our expectant little trio and switched itself on.

It took a while for the picture tube to warm up; exact duplication can sometimes have its disadvantages. Meanwhile, the speaker, after a preparatory tapping and breathing sound, issued a polite request for the few other people in the room besides the three of us to leave.

There were a few hoots and catcalls from the departing group, mostly to the effect that we had become victims of the plotters of Madison Avenue and the Establishment brain-drainers, but finally the pad was empty except for the four of us—Chester, Michael, my uncertain self, and what was, for present purposes, a 3V set of no particular make or model.

What with these little encounters with a lamp and a vacuum cleaner, and having to help drudge our erstwhile guests out of the various nooks and crannies of the pad, Mike and Chester were by now almost as down as my vidip call had taken me; not, I had to admit, that there was any indication that being straight was helpful during discussions with Alien pseudo-3V sets.

The 3V coughed experimentally while doing a slow 360° rotation. When the screen faced us again, it suddenly lit up with a lovely kaleidoscopic design in a sort of *art-nouveau* style.

"My name," the 3V announced, "is Solidus Plim."

16

There's this game they have in the newspapers; letters of a word are all scrambled up and the object of the puzzle is to rearrange them in their proper order. Quite often it will happen that you're looking at the letters, completely baffled, and they'll suddenly seem to just jump into your mind, changing places to form the word of their own accord—with no conscious help from you.

That was the sort of feeling I had now. A number of things were falling into place and a pattern-maybe *their* Pattern—was gradually making itself visible.

"Of course," the 3V continued, "I realize that this will mean nothing to you, but while my name is unimportant the information I must give you is vital to the security of your world."

"We're quite ready to listen," Mike said casually, "and I must say I'm beginning to see why your brother officers consider you a security risk."

The 3V did its version of blanching, and Mike was somewhat pleased. After all, it's something of an accomplishment to be able to one-up an Alien from an advanced race in the first exchange of a conversation. "How did you know that?" the 3V queried shakily, a green-on-blue pattern of question marks appearing on its screen.

"We know a few things," I said, "about what's been going on, for example that a guy named Jake Sheba is the contact for the invasion force—but we have more questions than answers so perhaps you'd better just go ahead with what you were going to tell us, and then we can proceed from there."

The screen faded to a lambent violet. "I'll do as you suggest," said the 3V in a slightly less-confident but at the same time relieved tone.

The violet gave way to a science-fiction movie view of a planet rotating slowly in space. It was the center of attraction for a four-sun system, and I would've hated to figure out the pattern of solar orbits that kept the planet in a stable position.

"This is Trisk, the home planet of my race," the 3V explained. "Less than twenty thousand of my—people—remain here, for though only a small number of us are required to subjugate a new world, this conquering is done on such a wide scale that most of us must be employed at it and far away from Trisk." The scene changed, and now we were looking at what was probably a city; it looked sort of like a transparent waterworks, with globs and streams of something opaque moving around at improbable angles and speeds through tubes and canals. "Our city," the 3V said succinctly (how clever of me!), and added, "There are several others on Trisk, but they are long since uninhabited. Here we live, and administrate the areas of the galaxy under our control."

The screen went back to a shifting abstract pattern. "Not long ago, in your relative measure of time, it was decided to bring your planet Earth under control of our Triskade Federation. A preliminary study had been made, during which contact had been achieved with a suitable Instigator, one whom you call Jake Sheba. From a judgment of this person as a random sample, and other considerations, there was a decision at our Council to invade."

At this point there were three thumps as our jaws hit the floor, but the 3V didn't seem to notice.

"I opposed this," it continued, "having doubts about the validity or usefulness of this continued aggression. In opposing it I was, of course, opposing the Pattern, and for a Triskan to do this was what you would call blasphemy."

"Don't feel bad," I interjected. "Most everyone on this planet is ready to kill and destroy for their local god."

"Yes," the 3V agreed, "and almost without exception, the other races and civilizations we have encountered have been quite ready to do violence of all kinds to their fellow sharers of life, so long as they could claim to be doing the will of a higher power, be it a god or a government."

"Depressing but very probable," said Chester.

"For my opposition," resumed the 3V, "I was placed in a Condition of Variance, and as a test of my loyalty to the Pattern was sent here. My superior officer has been watching me closely, and therefore until very recently I have been proceeding with standard duties of duplication and replication. In the course of this I discovered that you three had substantially correct suspicions concerning our phenomena, and therefore determined to contact you."

"Why'd you wait until now?" asked Mike.

The 3V turned slightly to face him directly. "I *did* try to make contact earlier, but was unsuccessful. After scanning your minds through the altered vidiphone of our Instigator, I selected an image that would intrigue one of you, and then at the proper time made encounter."

The pattern faded again, and as the new picture became visible there were snortings, horkings, and other sounds issuing from the general area of Mike. We were looking at a street scene: Michael plodding along Houston Street with a resigned expression, and about three paces behind him an eight-foot-tall teddy bear in Smokey guise.

"*You* were the one!" Mike managed to gasp.

"Of course," said the 3V equably. "What else could it possibly have been?" This didn't seem like quite a fair question, under the circumstances, and we all passed on it for the present.

The 3V moved back to its central position, and as the lovely image of Mike-pursued-by-bear faded back to abstract colors it continued speaking. "I had unfortunately miscalculated to a slight degree and your reactions were more extreme than I had expected. Even the use of the appropriate name failed to produce a response I could trust, and later circumstances did not permit the proper situation for me to impart the information I had obtained.

"Because of the numerous other Triskans in the Test Area, I had no opportunity to try contact again until this evening, and even that was delayed because of the presence of another Triskan here until a short time ago."

My Null-Wendy. Of course I had to ask. "What sex was this Triskan?"

"Sex?" the 3V echoed. The screen went completely blank for a few seconds and then the question marks appeared again.

"Skip it," I said. Well, if this story ever got out I supposed I'd be branded for life as a parasexual.

"You keep mentioning information you wanted to give us," Mike said changing the subject. "What exactly is it?"

The 3V seemed as relieved as I was. "Once I was assigned specific Pattern duties," it explained, "naturally I had to know at just what progression and grid the operation was positioned. Without going into the details, I will state that all of our operations—invasions—must follow the Pattern, and once the grid applicable to the situation has been determined, all progressions of the operation are set and ordered. What this means is simply that I can inform you of all succeeding moves our Triskan force will make."

Mike, as a student of military strategy and tactics, was cut to the quick, and his quick had lately become extremely sensitive. "You mean," he goggled, "that the Triskans use the *same* operation *everywhere* and *every time*? And it never fails?"

"The Pattern has not failed yet," responded the 3V quietly, "and whether it does now is entirely in your hands."

We were all quiet then. After a while Chester said, "Perhaps you'd better describe just what this pattern for conquest *is.*"

The 3V agreed. "In human terminology," it said, "the Pattern can be described very simply. The target planet having been selected and an Instigator—in your case Mr. Sheba—having been chosen, scanning mechanisms are suitably disguised and set in operation. With this information, duplication and replication of the life form and related artifacts is begun. The next stage involves continued dupli-replication, except now the familiar objects or beings are out of scale and other objects or beings are unfamiliar as a part of reality; these latter are generally drawn from myth or fable, which is usually available.

"This is done on a limited basis. The next and terminal stage is simply this same thing, but done on a Saturation basis through the entire Test Area."

"Well?" I asked after a long pause. "What then?"

The 3V registered its version of surprise. "That is the terminal phase," it repeated. "When it has been completed the target planet is under Triskade control."

We must have missed something.

17

W e must have missed something," the three of us cried in atonal chorus. The 3V was unimpressed by all this solidarity.

"What is your difficulty?" it asked, while the screen produced soothing undulations of design in muted colors.

Mike, as our Chief of Staff For Operations and Planning, got that one. "We just don't quite see how what you've just described would conquer a planet. Could you give us a little more detail on what actually happens?"

The 3V sighed. "My description seemed clear enough to me," it said petulantly, "but if you wish I shall try to be more explicit." The 3V paused for several seconds, presumably framing its thoughts into a context that would be elementary enough for even such cretins as its present audience to understand.

Finally it spoke up. "The purpose of the Pattern, which is infallible, is to produce events that will not correlate with the target peoples' systems and structures of reality. When such events have been clearly established in their minds as actually occurring, while impossible in their framework of knowledge, the people have one of two reactions: either they feel they can no longer interpret reality correctly—that is to say, that they are not sane—or they are made aware of the extreme limitations of their concepts of what they had previously considered to be reality. Which of these two reactions a being in this situation may select is of minor importance, for the end result is the same: they are totally confused and helpless, feeling completely unable to deal with the real world."

Sinister and cynical, but still . . .

"And then?" I prodded.

"And then," said the 3V, "after the Test Area has been extended to Full Pattern—the entire planet—and there is mass confusion, fear, and uncertainty, the Triskade Federation makes its official arrival. We restore order and calm, usually being viewed as the salvation of the world we've conquered, and along with the order and calm we produce a planet under our complete control. It takes some worlds a surprisingly long time to realize they've been conquered rather than saved."

We all thought about this one for a while, and the silence was longer than usual. Then Chester said, "Not to belabor the obvious, then, but what you're saying is that you Triskans have snatched planet after planet simply by putting the inhabitants out of touch with reality?"

"Briefly put, that is correct, yes," affirmed the 3V.

"Mother of God," breathed Chester, and then all three of us were whooping hysterically, rolling on the floor and beating it with our fists in helpless glee.

The 3V, alarmed by this incomprehensible reaction, had retreated to some distance during our collective fit, and only after we had subsided to wheezes, giggles, and snorts did it cautiously roll forward again. "I cannot correlate your response to my information," it said carefully.

"It's a little difficult to explain to someone who hasn't been living in the Village," I answered between giggles, and then the logical question to ask now lit up in my head. "What would happen," I queried, "if the Triskans went completely through the Pattern procedure and, well, nothing happened? There was no reaction?"

I could see that this was a tough theological question; little geometrical designs started appearing on the screen—they'd waver for a few seconds and then distort and twist up in ways I'd rather not describe even if I could. (Try to think of an isosceles triangle getting its neck broken and you will understand the difficulty.)

"There has never been such an occurrence, not in all the annals of the Pattern," the 3V said thoughtfully. "In the event that such a thing *did* happen, it would be interpreted as a flaw in the application of the Pattern, and the Test Area group would return to Trisk to analyze the situation and discover this flaw."

"And if no flaw could be found?" I continued probing.

"Then—there would be no further applications of the Pattern until this contradiction could be resolved. Quite probably a majority of captured worlds would be returned to the control of their own peoples, since the Triskans would feel it unwise to maintain a federation based on a premise no longer fully explainable or predictable."

The Triskan philosophy seemed to err on the side of caution—*way* on the side of caution. "How would you feel if that happened?" Chester asked.

Now the patterns on the screen started taking on a schmaltzy tinge. "Such a change would be my fondest wish," the 3V sighed, "but I realize that it is not possible. Nothing could so defy the Pattern."

Mike whooped again. "There are more things in Heaven and the Village," he chortled, "than are dreamt of in your philosophy."

If Solidus Plim, in his 3V guise, was playing it straight with us (and there was no reason to believe otherwise), it appeared that the world in general, the Village specifically, and we in particular had lucked out again. The Triskan Pattern being what it was, they could have landed just about anywhere on this tired old Earth without having much chance of succeeding. They depended on separating people from reality but, as a number of observers have pointed out,* not too long after we'd entered the atomic age our world became a place where reality and actuality were studiously avoided as a matter of preference, and the word *insanity* no longer had any meaning or relevance except as an archaic legalism that should have been edited even from the lawbooks.

But we couldn't have archaic and edit too.

The Triskans, however, had had doubly worse luck; first they had made a random selection of Instigator and picked the plum of all time, Mystic Jake—and then they had decided on Greenwich Village and environs as their Test Area. Jake was

---

* Notably R. D. Laing in his *The Politics of Experience.*

about as unreal as you could get and still be perceptible; and the existence of the Village in the world of actuality, as Chester pointed out in the Foreword to *The Butterfly Kid*, has always been highly questionable.

The closing stages of the Pattern would certainly be interesting.

The 3V was still radiating doubt and puzzlement, so for a while we tried to soothe it with various sociological observations about the Village. Finally it calmed down enough to inform us that, among other things, the limited part of the Pattern was drawing to a finish; tomorrow would be the beginning of Maximum Saturation. "Groovy," we said.

I also managed to find out, during all this, that my finally-remembered dream, the one I'd had after touching the live wire at the rear of Mystic Jake's vidiphone, hadn't been a dream at all. It had happened exactly as I had experienced it, to Solidus Plim himself, shortly before he'd been sent here. The final part, the feeling of changing, had been where my own mind took over again from the false memory. We theorized that the transporting circuits added to the vidiphone had, because of Plim's defiance of the Pattern, retained an impression of his vivid memory of the occurrence, and I'd somehow triggered it off when I shorted out the device.

When Plim found this out his attitude toward me changed for, just as he had been able to experience human form, I had, however subjectively, been able to feel how it was to be a Triskan.

Mike figured that the same basic property of the circuitry had been at the root of our adventure with Altamont and our brief subsequent dislocations; in this case, however, the deciding factor had been some sort of feedback to our own minds. It didn't take too much imagination to figure out that, as we skulked around Jake's pad in search of clues, little images of the Great Detective were pacing along the backs of our minds. We haven't yet quite figured out where we picked up on Count Dracula; none of us, so far, have admitted anything . . .

The dawn's ugly light was beginning to filter down the airshaft outside the windows by the time we were finished, more or less, with hashing and hassling things out. The only question that bothered us particularly was why Null-Wendy had made the

Toklas-brownie scene at the party, not to mention the T. Waters scene (I wasn't about to bring *that* up again.).

Solidus Plim had no answers for us on that one, but he promised to look into it; now he had to report back to his Base of Operations so that hopefully little would be suspected.

We watched as the 3V shimmered, wavered, and then lost shape and color as it began to elongate. The surfaces began to turn in on themselves in a way that pulled at our eyes, and then . . .

. . . we were looking at the archetypal Bowery derelict, so perfectly done and carefully detailed that we instinctively pretended not to notice him. He shuffled to the door and opened it, trailing unspeakable odors, and looked back at us with unfocused bleary eyes.

"Remember," he slurred, "the Pattern goes to Full Saturation at 3:00 p.m." Then, coughing and mumbling, he continued his shuffle down the hall and out the front door.

"Wow," I breathed softly. It had certainly been an impressive exit.

Well, we had an edge now, if one were needed; we had an agent in the enemy camp, just as the Triskans did—but ours, I could safely say, was a little more on the ball than theirs, and we *knew* about Mystic Jake, while they might only have unverifiable suspicions about Solidus Plim.

For a short while we tried to formulate an appropriate procedure for the Main Event in the afternoon, but it soon became evident that we were all a bit too strung out to make any sense. A bit of sleep was the essential thing now, and the world would just have to wait.

18

We more or less dropped in our tracks, and I was conscious of zero ought *nothing* for some time; then a hellish din gradually worked its way down into my brain, and as I awakened I interpreted the racket as the Midtown Wake-up Service, a vidip service staffed by sadists, with whom Mike had prudently placed a call for 11:00 a.m. I got up and toddled in to see what was happening.

Mike was standing in front of the vidip. A pretty girl who must've been nursed on amphetamine was smiling brightly and saying, "Rise and *Shine,* Mr. Garland, Rise and *Shine!*" Mike was staring at her in dazed incomprehension, as though she'd just suggested a perversion he'd never heard of for motives that were suspect.

I nudged Mike and he moved to one side without for an instant taking his eyes from the screen. It took a while to accept the call—the chick was very gung ho and emphatic about it being for *Mr. Garland*—but she finally conceded the match to me and switched out.

The screen going dark snapped Mike out of trance. "What time is it?" he asked.

"A little after eleven."

"Rrmph. I was supposed to get a wake-up call from my service. Can't depend on anything any more."

"Uh—Mike—" I explained.

By the time I'd convinced him that he'd answered their call, Chester was awake and ready for the big day. Over breakfast, which consisted of what was left from the party, we considered various ideas, and we're still not quite sure which one of us came up with what we finally used. We all claim it or disclaim it, depending on whom we're talking to.

Once we had our plan of action, Chester got on the vidip to an offset printer friend and people he knew at the FM stations. Mike and I, meanwhile, set out for the Midway. At this particular time of the year MacDougal would be pretty well crowded even this early in the day.

Solidus Plim had assured us, when questioned, that Full Saturation meant that the strange things happened wherever there were people. "Like a gathering in that park you have—the one named after a President."

"We had a President Central?" I had responded; that's how tired *I'd* been.

But Plim's descriptive example had planted a seed, which now had flowered its own little plot. Mike and I, separately, went into such coffee houses and the like as were available, and made our little announcement. At first a good number of the local crowd, who'd been victims of our put-on at one time or another, were skeptical; but then they started hearing the same announcement on the radio, and not long after that Chester arrived with the handbills, and we were hooked.

The handbill said:

K.A.W. PRODUCTIONS
a subsidiary of Warlock Associates
IS PROUD TO ANNOUNCE
THEIR WONDERFUL NEW INVENTION
a
BOON TO ALL MANKIND:
THE INCREDIBLE

HALLUCITRON

GUARANTEED TO PRODUCE VISIONS AND ILLUSIONS SUPERIOR
TO THOSE CREATED BY ANY KNOWN PHARMACOLOGICAL
SUBSTANCE!!!
DEMONSTRATION TODAY! THREE P.M. SHARP!
DEMONSTRATION TODAY!
WASHINGTONSQUAREPARKWASHINGTONSQUARE
PARKWASHINGTONSQUAREPARK
WASHINGTONSQUAREPARK
WASHINGTONSQUAREPARK

It was a very pretty handbill, and we hoped devoutly that it was telling what would later appear to be the truth; if Plim had given us a bum steer and the Triskans didn't show up, our poultry was definitely poached.

It took less time than we'd expected to distribute the handbills; after that, all that was left for Chester and me was to go over to the Square and wait for Mike, who had one additional job to do.

He did it very well, too, but it took him a while, and Chester and I were getting a bit edgy when Mike reappeared at about ten minutes to Zero hour. He exhibited his handiwork and whispered, "What do you think of the wonderful Hallucitron?"

It was impressive. Starting with an old attaché case, Mike had stuck a battery inside it and hooked it up to whatever spare electronic parts he could find—and he'd been able to find several of them. It clicked and whirred and flashed in grand abandon, and Mike hadn't even turned it on yet.

At one minute of three there must have been four thousand people in the Square, and every last one of them was looking at us, either furtively or openly. Mike wanted to make a speech to the expectant mob, but I pointed out that we didn't have time. Also I didn't think we should push our luck.

Precisely at three, with various bells tolling away, Mike threw the switch on the Hallucitron; the crowd oohed and aahed, and the Hallucitron began to whistle and flash and buzz and vibrate and otherwise enjoy itself.

Nothing else happened.

It only took our recruited mob about thirty seconds to realize that the Hallucitron itself was rather monotonous to watch, and then they looked round and discovered that there wasn't anything else to watch, either.

They began to mutter Carthaginian war chants and move toward us with expressions of abiding disapprobation. We might have had an unpleasant time of it except for the opportune arrival of a squad of mounted policemen. They faced the crowd with stern glares, and their unicorns waved their horns threateningly.

Ah.

We were at the Stone Ring, *nee* fountain, in the center of the Square, and it was a lovely vantage point for the proceedings of the afternoon.

From the midst of the crowd appeared helmeted and armored knights (we have a lot of romantics in the Village), who challenged the policeman to do battle. It went very evenly for a while, and then when the policemen seemed to be losing they suddenly disappeared, to be replaced by a flock of pterodactyls which immediately took to the air.

The pterodactyls didn't seem much interested in the knights; they spent most of their time having midair battles with each other that would have warmed the heart of a Baron Von Richtofen. The knights, apparently feeling unwanted, disappeared, and in their place were the Children of Bacchus, handsome boys and sensuous girls, all dressed either in nothing or as near to it as made no difference. There seemed to be more than enough of them for all practical purposes, and said purposes were quickly discovered as they moved into the crowds and people discovered they were pleasantly solid and real.

The scene that ensued when this was generally known looked like a 3D Cinerama spectacle based on the *Kama Sutra* and *Ananga Ranga*. At first I wasn't quite sure how to react, since I knew the true nature of these love-children, but then I found myself between two impossibly sensual females, faultless of form and fanatically lustful . . .

Well, if it *feels* like it . . .

. . . *looks* like it . . .

. . . *tastes* like it . . .

. . . as the old auctioneers used to say, call it what you want and use it for the same purpose. It was a while before I was sufficiently in command of my attention to take a look at the present stage of things.

A squad of *real* policemen had tried to enter the park, but the Bacchantes had intercepted them and stopped them, so to speak, in their tracks. Mike was nearby, barely visible beneath a bare-ass mint of female riches, and the Hallucitron was chugging happily to itself.

It took a bit longer to spot Chester. He had climbed up onto the large concrete base for the flagpole, and was conducting a one-hundred-seventy-six-piece orchestra, of which a hundred-and-seventy-five were Chester playing the sopranino recorder; the other one was Chester too, but playing counterpoint on the bassoon.

The Hallucitron finally giggled inanely and died, but no one seemed to notice, least of all Mike. Forty-nine sets of the Seven Dwarfs moved through the crowd telling them about it, but nobody cared.

The Seven Dwarfs got disgusted and, pulling out bows and arrows, started shooting down the pterodactyls. The reptiles crashed to the ground with horrendous thuds, but the only effect this seemed to have on them was to change them to pterodactyl pie. A freshly-baked greenish smell drifted by, and a stampede of Chester's orchestra followed swiftly, all of them evidently having a passion for pterodactyl pie.

A gang of teen-age thugs appeared briefly—a reasonable percentage of the crowd probably had this paranoia—but the Dwarfs outnumbered them; they became overchromed motorcycles and beat a hasty retreat.

My pet Bacchantes were at me again, and I don't know what else was happening for the next little while. Presently, however, the tenor of the phenomena shifted; the Children of Bacchus thinned out and disappeared, followed by the Seven Dwarfs and all but a couple of the pterodactyls. Chester's orchestra had disappeared imperceptibly earlier, and now for about ten minutes or so things were quiet.

Then it began to rain tennis balls.

This was an interesting effect, considering its attendant technical problems, and I was quite impressed with it; most of the crowd was just baffled, and stood there uncertainly until they were waist-deep in tennis balls. The spheroid rain stopped abruptly, nothing happened for a minute or so, and then the balls began to melt and evaporate; in less than thirty seconds there was no trace of them.

Nothing happened now for nearly a half-hour, and then shortly after dusk came the final effort: a monster appeared.

Boy, did a monster appear!

It was suddenly just *there,* crouched in a close fit beneath Washington Square Arch. It had several hundred eyes, and none of them were friendly.

Huge tentacles twined from its waist like a sentient hula skirt; behind them, three beak-like mouths could be seen, snapping spasmodically and drooling. Its legs were the size of tree trunks, and twined in the slimy hair that covered them were fragments of human bones. The feet had razor-edged yellow claws, more than I cared to count.

The monster took a few steps forward, and its pulsating head moved from side to side. Then it gave a long roar, a sound roughly like a train wreck.

For a long moment, then, there was silence; and then the whole Square broke up into hysterical laughter.

It was just too overdone; the thing was so monstrous that it *wasn't*—only ridiculous, like a ham actor taking ten minutes for a death scene. It was the funniest thing we'd ever seen.

The monster stood in the face of this hilarity for only a few moments; then it was gone, and the Park grew quiet, and evening had come.

The Park was empty now, except for the three of us and the dead Hallucitron. Everything had gone well, but somehow it didn't feel complete.

Mike put his finger on the trouble. "One person we know was conspicuous by his absence. Shame, isn't it?"

Chester and I agreed. It really wasn't fair to leave Mystic Jake out of all the fun. "Perhaps," said Chester, "we should drop by and tell him what he missed."

Frantic conversation and other odd sounds drifted out to us, presently, we were at the door of Mystic Jake's pad. It was wide open, and Jake took no notice of our presence. He had other problems.

"Hey, now, lissen, man! Lissen, y'gotta believe me, y'gotta try this thing again . . . hey, man, c'mon, it'll work, y'just have to do it once more . . . hey?" Poor Jake: he was a compulsive sellout with no buyers.

"I have already explained," said the Dwarf, "that such a course as you suggest is impossible. The Pattern has failed to operate properly and nothing more can be done unless the Flaw can be ascertained. We are returning to Trisk."

"Aw, hey, c'mon—" Jake began with his severely limited bleat.

The Dwarf caught sight of us and cut him off in mid-whine. "No further discussion," it said sharply. "If it is really necessary for you to know why, however, I suggest you ask these gentlemen." Aha, it was Solidus Plim.

Mystic Jake spun around as though on a spring, and when he saw us he turned the color of old and dirty milk. "Uh, uh, hey—hey, now," he was trying, "—uh, whadayou want with me?" Instant guilt.

"We just thought you might want a report on what you helped plan, you *reject* from a slime factory," I said.

"Didn't turn out quite as you'd expected, did it?" asked Chester, who was enjoying himself hugely.

Mike enjoys the sinister parts. He finished our little speech with, "We'll tell you all about it, Jake, old boy, and then we'll figure out some suitable reward." Lovely tone of menace, just lovely.

Mystic Jake backed away from us toward the vidiphone; he gave the effect of being slowly disassembled from the inside. "Hey, now, lissen," he said desperately, "lissen, I was really tryna *stop* 'em, no really, lissen, I was, I swear I was gonna stop 'em, really, may I burn in Hell forever if I ain't—"

ZZAP!

I began to have doubts about my feelings on religion; Jake had disappeared—completely gone he was, and there was a slight burning smell.

"However did you manage that?" marveled Chester, and the Dwarf shook his head.

"I had nothing to do with that," he insisted. "Most probably he brushed against that shorted wire and somehow activated the transporter circuits."

"I wonder," I said dreamily, "if that effect occurred and he went to where he was thinking about just then."

The Dwarf shrugged, and looked at each of us in turn. Then, without a word, he turned to the vidip and punched a button. Instantly he began to melt and shrink, and then we were alone in the room.

So that's how we saved the world for the third time—really, that's exactly how it happened; don't pay any attention to what Mike and Chester say—that's really the way it was.

The vidip in Mystic Jake's pad no longer did anything unusual, or usual, for that matter; it didn't work at all—and just a while ago Mike called to report that Jake's pad had been gutted by a fire, destroying everything.

If I were my old, confident self, the finality of that news would have been enough for me to state that our adventures had reached

THE END

but these days, as *you* should know, you never can tell . . .